DEEP
GIRLS

Lori Weber

DEEP
GIRLS

The publisher gratefully acknowledges the support of the Canada Council for the Arts and
the Ontario Arts Council for its publishing program. We acknowledge the financial support
of the Government of Canada through the Canada Book Fund (CBF) for our publishing
activities, and the Government of Ontario through the Ontario Media Development
Corporation, an agency of the Ontario Ministry of Culture, and the Ontario Book
Publishing Tax Credit Program.

LIBRARY AND ARCHIVES CANADA CATALOGUING IN PUBLICATION

Weber, Lori, 1959–, author
Deep girls / Lori Weber.

Short stories.
Issued in print and electronic formats.
ISBN 978-1-77086-531-0 (softcover). — ISBN 978-1-77086-532-7 (HTML)
I. Title.

PS8645.D24D44 2018   JC813'.6   C2018-903806-3
                            C2018-903807-1

United States Library of Congress Control Number: 2018946339
Cover design: angeljohnguerra.com
Interior text design: Tannice Goddard, bookstopress.com

Printed and bound in Canada.
Printer: Sunville Printco.

DCB
An imprint of Cormorant Books Inc.
260 Spadina Avenue, Suite 502, Toronto, Ontario, M5T 2E4
www.dcbyoungreaders.com

For my mom, Maureen,
the most deeply beautiful and
beautifully deep woman I know, with love.

CONTENTS

DEEP
GIRLS

DEEP
GIRLS

"**Y**ou can buy clothes to hide *that*, Lizzie," my
mother says, pointing to my stomach, like she
can't say the word. She has told me many times that the
only time she had a stomach was after she had me, but
sit-ups took care of the bulge pretty fast — one hundred
a day. She still does them, sixteen years later. When I
catch her, I imagine her chanting, *A hundred a day keeps
the flabbies away*, a perversion of Huxley's, *A soma a day
keeps the jim-jams away*.

"And your skin ..." she continues, patting her own
cheeks, as though our skin is connected. My mother is
the regional rep for MoDerm, a natural skincare line
that originated on a farming co-op in Vermont. Skin is
her life.

"You want me to hide my face, too?" I ask.

"No, silly. The pimples." She pronounces the p's hard, spitting them out, like seeds. My mother didn't have pimples at my age. Her old pictures prove it. Besides, if one had sprouted, she'd have attacked it, full-force, with creams and potions. My mother is like the Joan of Arc of beauty. Even now, at seven a.m., she's wearing an elegant satin housecoat and has already brushed her hair and pampered her face. She's sipping green tea, because its anti-oxidants are good for aging. MoDerm products are supposedly full of them.

"That stuff I bought you, with zinc and cinnamon," she says, "have you tried it?"

I gulp down the rest of my coffee, shake my head, and walk away. That lotion, along with all the other MoDerm products she has given me over the years, made with honey or dandelion root or witch hazel, are sitting, unused, on my bureau.

To tell you the truth, between my mother and Joe, I get more advice on how to improve my looks than I can stand. They just don't seem to get that my body isn't my main priority. Not in the same way Joe's body is for him. That's because he's a runner. He runs for an hour before school and an hour after school. Sometimes he even runs at lunch. Before he became my boyfriend, I used to watch him run the track behind the school. I thought he was kind of cute, in a rugged sort of way, but he wasn't the type of guy I usually talked to.

"Why don't you join me?" he asked one day.

"Because I hate running," I said, moving on. After that, the more I watched, the harder Joe ran, like he was giving me a private performance. Eventually, he'd run past me as I was walking home, doing each block three times for my one time, looping around me like a cattle rancher rounding up his steer. Finally, he began waiting at the foot of my driveway, running on the spot. He became extremely hard to avoid.

"I'll take you to a movie Friday," he said one day, as though I'd asked him to and he was now accepting my offer.

"And who says I want to go?" I replied. It sort of amazed me that Joe was after me. I'm not what guys call 'hot.' I'm not ugly, but I guess I'm pretty plain. My mother always tells me I have great potential, if only I'd put in the effort.

But Joe just shrugged, ran on the spot, exaggerating his knee lifts, and took off. "I'll pick you up at eight."

At the theatre, we couldn't agree on a movie. I wanted to see *Jane Eyre*, but Joe had his heart set on the latest *Batman*. In the end, Joe won out. I couldn't stand the thought of someone rolling their eyes and yawning over Jane Eyre, the proud governess whom Rochester falls in love with, despite her plain exterior. Even now, I like to picture Charlotte Brontë writing the book with a quill, tucked away in her little country parsonage, surrounded by the mysterious English moors that she and her sisters were always roaming in.

"There. That wasn't so bad, was it?" Joe said on our way out of the theatre. "Lots of action, not like a chick-flick." I couldn't tell if he was teasing, he had this way.

"You know, *Jane Eyre* has action too," I replied. "There's a mad woman locked up in an attic, attempted murders, arson." But Joe didn't respond. Maybe he didn't believe me.

At my place, Joe kissed me goodnight. He was wearing a track jacket made of slippery nylon. When I tried to put my hand on his shoulder it slid right off. I could feel my mother in the house, anxiously waiting to hear about my first date. She had tried to talk me into putting on some make-up before leaving. And she had even chosen clothes for me to wear, my tightest and most revealing. I wore them, but covered up the top with a baggy jean shirt, just to show her I didn't care.

Joe and I have now been going out for a whole month and he's still trying to talk me into running with him.

"Come on, Lizzie, it would be fun," he says.

"No thanks. I hate sports," I always reply.

"Sports are good for you, better than reading," Joe

says, hitting a sore spot. I love to read. I finish at least one, maybe two, novels per week. I've been working my way through the alphabet of classics, author by author. So far, I've read *The Mill on the Floss* by George Eliot. Before that I read *Oliver Twist* by Charles Dickens, *The Plague* by Albert Camus, *Wuthering Heights* by Emily Brontë and *Pride and Prejudice* by Jane Austen. The books belonged to my grandmother, who left them to me in her will. They have gold lettering down the spines and black and white drawings on onion paper inside.

"You read too much. You'll ruin your eyes," Joe says.

"Yeah, well, you run too much. You'll ruin your feet."

"You don't know what you're talking about. You don't just use your feet to jog. You use everything — your knees, your thighs, your hips, your arms, your lungs, and especially your heart."

"Yeah, well, reading involves way more than your eyes." I want to tell Joe that reading touches your brain, your soul, and especially your heart. But I don't. He'd only roll his eyes.

"Deep girls are no fun," Joe says, a smile curling the corner of his lips. "You ought to lighten up, like your mother." Then he begins to do the leg stretches that signify the start of another run. Even if I could respond to this blow it would be tough because one minute his face is beside mine, the next it's down around my ankles.

I think about breaking up with Joe a lot, but the trouble is this: my parents love him. The first time they met, my mother ushered Joe into the living room and practically pushed him onto our sofa. Then she handed him a glass of white wine, even though he's only seventeen. Later, she pulled me into the kitchen and told me Joe was a dish. God! What a word. It made me think of Joe's head on a silver platter, like John the Baptist's.

When we returned to the living room, Joe and my father were deep in conversation.

"We'll have to put you on the bike, Joe. See how far you can go," my father was saying. My father is obsessed with cycling. He cycles a hundred miles a week minimum, in good weather. In the winter, he cycles in the basement on a stationary bike while watching travel videos. I think he really believes he's biking around the Pyrenees because he'll lean his whole body into the curves of the roads that the camera is following.

I thought Joe would need rescuing, but the next thing I knew, they were fixing a date.

The following Saturday my father took Joe to Oka and back, a ride of about seventy-five miles. My father was very impressed by Joe's condition.

"You kept up well, there, Joe," he said, putting his arm around Joe's shoulder and ushering him past me into the house.

My mother had lemonade ready. I was afraid it might be spiked with vodka. According to MoDerm philosophy, a tiny amount of alcohol stimulates blood flow which cleanses the skin — but never more than a touch.

"Your dad is amazing," Joe said. "I hope I'm in that kind of shape when I'm older." I could see my father beaming. This was what he'd always wanted — an eager child to share his passion for sports. He'd been trying for years to get me out on the bike with him, to help control what he calls my 'weight problem.' I tried to flash Joe a sympathetic smile, but couldn't. My mouth just froze in an awkward expression. I tried not to let it show, but as my parents and Joe talked, I couldn't stop thinking about Neil, this guy in my English class that I'd run into at the park earlier that day. We'd sat on a bench and, before I knew it, we were deep in conversation about the war in Syria. Then we talked about how conservative politicians don't even believe in global warming, even though the polar ice caps are melting. I could never talk to Joe about any of those things.

Since that day, Joe's gone cycling with my father almost every weekend. Sometimes, he comes over to our house in the evening and my father joins him for a run.

"Break a leg," my mother calls after them, laughing hard, as though she has just said the wittiest thing in the world.

As I watch their two bodies growing smaller and smaller down the road, bobbing up and down like far-away insects, I try to sort out how I feel about Joe. I think about how he slaps my thighs and teases me when they ripple. Once, he slapped my bum and said it felt like a bowl of Jell-O. My parents laughed at that one, but I could see my mother cringe, as though she couldn't believe she was related to someone with Jell-O-bum.

I know I should break up with Joe, but I'm afraid my parents will give me a hard time if I do. They'll go on and on about what a fool I am to the point where I'll feel like I'm breaking up a happy family. So, I just let things continue, as if I don't really have the power to stop them. Joe grows closer and closer to my parents as I read further and further into the classics, finally hitting Flaubert.

"You should get a layered cut and have some highlights put in," my mother advises me one afternoon while I'm lying on my bed reading *Madame Bovary*. I know my straight, plain brown hair drives my mother crazy. She doesn't actually use the word "mousy," but I can feel her thinking it.

"I mean, it would add some body," she continues, bouncing her own hair as she says this. My mother dyes her hair on a regular basis. Whenever I watch her hang her head over the bathtub and rub in the chemical solution, being careful not to let it drip into her eyes, I feel sorry for her hair. I believe hair should just be allowed to be, naturally, instead of getting assaulted by toxic dye every six weeks, totally against its will.

"Yeah, well, my hair's okay as it is," I say, without looking up. I don't want to see the expression on her face. If my grandmother were here she'd help me out. She'd gone white at forty, her hair soft as a baby's. My mother thought it was a disgrace.

"All I'm saying is you could put in a bit more effort. You have such a great guy there. You'll lose him if you don't."

The real reason for her annoyance is that Joe is taking me out tonight to meet his entire family, including some American cousins, but I haven't been able to put down my book. Madame Bovary is just about to plunge into her affair with Léon. She's weighing the pros and cons. Personally, I hope she'll go for it. She and that drip of a doctor husband have absolutely nothing in common.

My mother keeps poking her head around my door to see if I'm moving yet. "His whole family will be there, Lizzie. First impressions and all that."

There's no way I can tell her I really don't want to go.

"Lizzie! Have some pride."

"Okay, okay," I say, finally. It's only four and we aren't leaving until six. I don't need two hours to get ready, but I'll pretend I do if it gets my mother off my back. I know that if I gave myself over to her, she'd cut, primp, pluck and color me up, making me over in her image, or in the image of what her ideal girl looks like.

∽

JOE'S FAMILY TAKES up three tables at an expensive steak restaurant that has a giant cow statue in the front lawn. The cow wears a sign, in the shape of cow bells, with the restaurant's name around its neck. The menu is white with black splotches all over it. When our steaks arrive, they're decorated with bits of parsley speared by toothpicks with cows at the top. Similar toothpicks stand in the baked potatoes, like cows in snow.

Joe introduced me to everyone back at his house before leaving, but I can't remember anyone's name.

"So, this is Joe's girlfriend," one of his cousins calls from across the table, as though he's just noticed me. "Hey, who would have thought Joe could get a girl to go out with him."

Everyone laughs, even Joe.

"How'd he sweep you off your feet there, Lizzie? Did he just scoop you up while running?" I envision Joe running with me in a wheelbarrow, my legs dangling over the sides.

"Oh, you know, it just kind of happened," I say.

"Joe says you're a real brain," another cousin chimes

in. "I wouldn't have thought anyone with a brain would go out with Joe. You should've known better."

His whole family cracks up. They think it's a joke, but when I look at Joe, I know they're probably right. Except I can't say that.

"Well?" Joe asks, staring at me, his fork frozen mid-air, and I realize he's waiting for me to say something witty in his defense.

"Oh, you know, Joe's not as dumb as he looks," I say, trying to sound playful. I wait for his cousins to laugh again, but they don't. They just look back and forth at each other and shrug.

I try to smile at Joe, but he just shoves a piece of steak into his mouth and concentrates on chewing. My stomach churns. If I were more like my mother, I would've said something charming, like, *Oh, it doesn't take brains to fall for someone like Joe, just great taste*. And then I would've fixed them with a flirtatious and silencing glance.

But I'm not my mother.

Nobody asks me another question.

I continue to eat, taking small, dainty bites so I can chew delicately, like my mom always does. It works, until I hit a piece of fat. It's one of those rubbery lumps, the kind you can't grind down, no matter how hard you try. Even mashing it between my molars has no effect. In fact, it's bigger than ever, like my chewing has expanded it. If I swallow it, I'll choke. I look around the table. Joe and his cousins seem to have forgotten me. They're lost in family stories, reminiscing about shared camping trips and eccentric relatives I'll never meet.

There's only one thing to do. I hold my cow napkin against my mouth and spit. Joe turns his head just in time to see the soggy lump fall out. He twists his face into an expression I've never seen on him before, his eyes narrowing to dark slits, his nose scrunching up. It's like he's chewing something disgusting too, something he'd like to spit out — the image of me, perfectly gross beside him. It's the same way my mom sometimes looks when she sees the way I dress, when she can't believe I'm her daughter.

I suddenly remember a story Neil told me that day in the park. He said that when he was little and his parents got into one of their big fights, he'd imagine himself retreating into a protective shell, like an egg. He'd literally feel himself curl up inside it and drift far away from the yelling and angry fists. He'd focus all his energy on keeping the shell intact, on not letting anything crack it. I remember how I had wanted to reach out and stroke his face when he told me.

Finally, Joe shakes his head and turns away. He doesn't

say it, but I know he regrets bringing me. I haven't made him shine in any way. I can hear his cousins, back at his house, asking him why he's going out with me, what he sees in me. And him shrugging, as if he can't explain it.

I retreat inside my own shell, blocking out the table and the clatter of dishes and the voices of Joe's family. I curl up, cozy and warm, until I'm only vaguely aware of the people around me pushing back their chairs, going up to the bar to buy drinks, or to dance on the dance floor that's under some beams made up to resemble a barn.

Suddenly, Joe's hand is reaching toward me. I see it at the same time as I think what an awfully long way it will have to travel and how strange it is that he's trying to touch me. But then his hand swerves behind me. He grabs the elastic that I used earlier to pull back my hair. My mother sighed when she saw me walk downstairs before leaving home. "You had two hours to get ready and all you could manage was a rubber band," she said.

Joe pulls firmly, sliding the elastic the length of my ponytail. A few hairs catch in the rubber and tug my scalp, then my limp hair falls to my shoulders.

"You should never wear your hair up," Joe says. "It doesn't suit you." Then he scrapes back his chair and runs over to the dance floor. I watch him tuck himself in between his cousins.

The shell around me cracks.

I stand alone beside the tables, two rows of dirty dishes stretching toward the window and then beyond it, their reflection floating outside in the dark. I'm there too, standing like a ghost on the other side of the glass.

I don't hesitate.

I bend down to retrieve my elastic from the floor. Several of my mousy brown hairs are still clinging to it. I pull them free and release them over Joe's plate, grinning as they sink into a puddle of gravy. I let another one fall into his glass of water, in case he's thirsty when he returns.

I feel my cellphone in my back pocket. If I call my mother, she'll come get me, but she'll hiss at me the whole way home.

So I decide to walk. I know the way and I'm not afraid of the dark. I'll pretend I'm Jane Eyre, wandering over the moors, breathing the night air deeply into my lungs.

I'll tie my hair back up as I go.

THE GIRL IN
THE PURPLE PANTS

I just handed in my composition. I've been sitting in class all afternoon, clutching it tightly between my fingers, trying to decide whether I'd actually do it or not, but just two seconds ago, the teacher pulled it out of my hand. I'll be in trouble now. Teen suicide is a hot topic these days. The school is always parading in experts to lecture us about it. They all say the same thing — to keep the lines of communication open. As if life is that easy. As if there is a permanent two-way conversation going on and all you have to do is keep the signal strong, without interference.

Anyway, it's done and I don't care. It already seems like ages ago that I wrote it, curled up in my private corner in the library. The words just fell out of me, as though

I were a tree and they were my apples, ripe and ready to eat. I hope the teacher chokes on them. She's always saying, "Wake up, Steph. You're on the moon." And then she'll roll her eyes and add, "Oh, whatever!" and wave me away. As if that's doing anything to keep the lines of communication open. My composition is peppered with mournful lines, like *The dark sleep of perpetual night will pull its shade over my soul* and *The cold and lonely nights will be my only companions.* I know they're corny, but they'll have an effect.

The topic was "Our Wish for the Future." Our teacher is expecting lots of science fiction stories about personal transport jets, computers small enough to fit onto rings, teleportation, those sorts of things. But the subject of my story is a pink pill, as tiny as a grain of sand, but powerful enough to make me disappear — not forever, but for the next few years, until I'm old enough to move out of my house and start an independent life.

"So, what 'ya write about?" Kayla, my best friend, asks me on the way out of class.

"I don't know, whatever," I answer, shrugging her off. I don't ask what she wrote because I know that it'll be something lovely and inspiring, like peace and goodwill for all mankind. That kind of thing.

"Want to come over?" she asks.

"No, I can't. I have too much homework," I lie. "Thanks, though."

When I see my geography teacher approaching, I duck into the washroom. She has asked me to stay after school twice this year. Both times she just sat beside me, staring, asking me if everything was all right. She said she could see so much going on behind my eyes in class, when I stared at the board or day-dreamed out the window. I wondered if my eyes were like a map to her and in them she saw lakes and rivers of tears, mountains of strength, and valleys of despair — all that poetic stuff. But I gave her nothing. I just kept insisting that everything was fine, until eventually she had to let me go.

Out in the school yard I automatically look for the girl in the purple pants. She came to our school two months ago and she's impossible to miss. I've never seen anyone wear pants that color to school before, and I don't understand how she gets away with it. We all have to wear uniforms: plain navy skirts with white blouses for the girls, navy pants and white shirts for the boys. The purple of her pants is the color of lilacs, the darker kind. It's also the same purple as the beautiful satin halter-top dress my mother gave my sister last summer, before my sister turned bad.

The girl with the purple pants never sits still. She's constantly spinning and twirling. Just now, she's bouncing out from the middle of a ball game. I watch her pirouette over to where the boys huddle, screaming, "You can't catch me." Then she takes off like a gazelle, lifting off the ground with a simple bend of the knees that sends her soaring. She is the freest person I've ever seen and I can't take my eyes off her.

As I walk home, I think of the questions the school counselor will ask me once my teacher hands over the composition. She'll pick and probe at me, like a lab rat. But the thing is this: if you've never experienced what it's like to walk into a house where everything feels wrong, where the only sound in the absolute quiet is the sound of your mother crying, then I can't explain it to you.

That day, I tiptoed up the fourteen stairs to find my mother curled in a ball in the corner of my sister's room, holding one hand very tenderly in the palm of the other. As I approached, I saw that the skin on her index finger was ripped open. A white bone poked through, curving up above her hand like a hook. Behind her, my sister's desk lamp lay on the floor, its coiled neck curved inward, its plastic head shattered. My sister, who had probably thrown it, was nowhere to be seen.

"Call an ambulance," my mother whimpered.

It was the very next day that the girl with the purple pants showed up, as if she'd been sent to divert me. Every time I saw the purple, I forgot the fact that my mother was still in the hospital. It had nothing to do with the finger. That was no big deal — a reset and a cast had fixed that. It was her head that needed healing.

And then the dumb composition. Well, I wrote what I wrote and I don't care. Let them call me in and question me. I'll tell them nothing. I'll roll my eyes and look at the ceiling the way I do at home to drive my mother crazy, now that she's so into discussing her feelings. On the road to recovery, the social worker calls it. I do it when my mother tries to get me to talk about how I feel about the fact that my sister no longer lives with us. She was taken away and put into something called a group home. The social worker who comes to visit gives us progress reports. And she tells my mother to encourage me to express my feelings.

"Don't let her bottle them up," I heard her say. "She needs to express herself or she may have problems later on."

Problems are one thing my parents can do without, now that the problem of my sister and her wild behavior has been taken care of. When the social worker refers to my sister's progress it makes me think of her as some sort of project, the type I used to do in elementary school, like a pioneer winter scene or teepee or igloo. My sister, the Styrofoam girl, with popsicle stick limbs, and cotton ball hair.

WHEN I GET home from school, my mother tells me that the social worker is coming over tonight to discuss my sister's situation. It seems that the group home she's in is what is called a transition house — it's a stepping stone on the way to somewhere more permanent. One of the options would be for her to come home.

"Do you love your sister?" the social worker, who wears too much perfume, asked me on her last visit. We were all assembled in the living room for a family therapy session. My mother and I sat on the sofa, the social worker on the armchair, with the round coffee table in between us. On it sat a plate of tea biscuits, but my mother had forgotten to make the tea. My father sat on a hard chair beside the door, twirling his tennis racket the whole time, as if he'd jump up any minute and run out to find a court.

We all turned beet red when she said the word "love" out loud. It seemed to hover in the air like a sudden dark cloud that appears from nowhere and threatens to drown a picnic. I could feel my parents and myself sitting with our breath sucked in, afraid to release it in case we made a sound by mistake.

I wanted to say yes, but the dead silence in the room prevented me. For a terrible second I thought, what if she's carrying a tape recorder in her fancy leather purse? What if her intention is to record this session to play back to my sister, to prove to her that she is loved, that we want her back?

All she would hear now was our embarrassed silence.

∽

THERE'S NO WAY I'm going to stick around for tonight's session. I'll sneak out before Miss Mazda comes. I call the social worker that because that's the type of car she drives, a bright red one. There's nothing discrete about her visits. She might as well hang a sign on our balcony that says, "screwed up family."

"Can't stay, Mom. Kayla and I have to finish our group project for tomorrow."

She frowns, but I know she believes me. I find this odd because chronic lying was one of my sister's talents. You'd think my mother would be more careful with me.

I watch the red Mazda pull up. As the social worker gets out, I step behind a bush to hide. If she sees me she'll want to wave me over and rescue me. Maybe she has a lasso hidden in her purse, ready to haul in needy teenagers.

I have about an hour to kill so I decide to just roam the neighborhood. It's seven o'clock and already dusky. In an hour it'll be pitch-black. I walk north, to a part of the neighborhood that borders the train tracks across from some clothing factories. It's a run-down area of chockablock apartment buildings with rusted, sagging balconies. The sidewalks are all cracked, with weeds sprouting up between them.

Just as I'm about to turn home, a door up the street flies open and three screaming kids run out onto the sidewalk, the two smallest in bare feet and pajamas. They run toward me then stop, huddling together, their arms linked around one another like a chain. A few seconds later a woman runs toward them, her arms flapping like wings. The children open the circle to let her in and she draws them to her protectively, pulling their heads toward her chest. She's crying, and in the light cast by a street lamp I can see that her face is very red and swollen, as though it has been beaten.

A few seconds later a police car pulls up and two officers disappear inside the building. A second car arrives and two more officers rush out to meet the mother and her children on the sidewalk. In what seems like no time at all, the door of the apartment building reopens and the first two officers emerge, supporting a man between them. His head is hung low, as though he's trying to bury it in his neck. The mother and her children instinctively huddle closer when he passes behind them. I can almost feel their arms grasp tighter. The police officers throw the man into the back of their car and drive off while the officers who are sheltering the group begin to lead them slowly back toward their apartment.

It's only after the circle breaks up that the lamp light catches the pants of the eldest child, illuminating the bright purple. Only it's no longer the purple of lilacs. It's the purple of a bruise, a deep dark bruise, the kind that flowers on the skin for a long time after it's been hurt.

The girl with the purple pants turns her head toward me. Even though the street is dark, her eyes hit mine dead on. She shoots me a long, piercing look. It's a look that tells me not just that she's sensed my presence, but that she's seen me watching her all these weeks. She's seen me sitting on the school stairs, following her wonderful freedom and lightness, her gazelle-like run and ballerina turns. And she has seen the envy in my eyes. Now, she's inviting me to see her again, to see her for real for the first time.

As her eyes hold mine on the near dark street I think that this is the clearest moment of communication I've ever experienced in my life. There's not a single drop of static on the line between us.

Next week, in English class, I receive a note from the counselor ordering me to see her immediately. I don't go to her office reluctantly. I don't have any master plan. I'll tell her whatever she wants to know. I'll tell her my sister is moving back home and I'm scared because I don't know what this means. There may be more fighting, more late-night shouting, more crying. All the way down the hall, I carry in my mind the picture of the new girl walking off on the dark street, her legs heavy as lead. Walking off to wherever. She never returned to school. Now I know she wouldn't have had time to buy the school uniform anyway. Her purple pants were her uniform. They gave her the illusion of lightness and freedom, because they were the color of wild flowers.

I turn the handle of the counselor's door and hear her phony, sweet voice call out, "Come on in, Steph."

The purple explodes in my mind like a bouquet.

CAPTIVITY

Miranda is sitting on a chair in Mitchell's living room, waiting for him. He said they were going to the beach, but for the last hour he's been sprawled out on the floor, watching reruns of *The Dukes of Hazard*. The small plastic table beside her is covered in junk. Miranda pushes an ashtray out of the way to make room for her towel and it falls, spilling butts and ashes at her feet. She sighs and leans back, hitting her head on the gold Buddha thermometer. The mercury in Buddha's belly has already risen to eighty degrees. Back home, in Toronto, spring would just be blooming, the crocuses in her parents' garden opening their lilac faces and the bushes that rim the stone-fronted house sprouting green buds. In a few weeks, the cherry tree would explode with pink blossoms. Miranda used to love that tree, even though the blossoms fell off after a week.

Mitchell's younger sister, Tillie, is rollerblading up and down the bare wood floors, lifting her arms over her head like a ballerina. She smashes into the coffee table, sending a stack of *National Enquirers* to the floor. Miranda can hear her mother exclaim that that is where such trash belongs. Her parents' bookshelves are filled with beautifully bound classics, like *Jane Eyre*, *Oliver Twist*, and *Huckleberry Finn*. All orphans, Miranda thinks, kind of like herself, except she has parents. She's just chosen not to live with them anymore. She now lives with Mitchell, his parents, Tillie and her twin brother Tyler, in Florida more than a thousand miles from home.

"Hey, get outta the way," Mitchell yells at Tillie, who's skating in front of the television, blocking the shot of Bo and Daisy. Before coming here, that old show had been Miranda's only exposure to the American south. She and her sister, Cordelia, used to mimic the sing-songy drawl of the characters.

"Gimme a haul," Tillie says, swiping Mitchell's cigarette from his hand.

"You little bitch," he calls after her. Tillie is thirteen, the same age as Cordelia. Miranda can't imagine her sister smoking, especially at home. Her parents would have a fit.

The smell of burned toast drifts down the hall and the wail of a country singer is drowned out by yells of "git lost, it's mine," along with the banging of cupboard doors. Miranda imagines the calm of the breakfast table back home, the glass jam dish with its wooden spoon being passed around, coffee percolating in its pot.

Tillie skates over Miranda's toes, snapping her painfully out of her daydream. "Ouch! Mitchell, I can't take this anymore." She marches outside and into Mitchell's old car. She can feel a headache coming on, and it isn't helped by the way Mitchell is now banging on the windshield.

"Hey, Miranda, come on, open up. I'm sorry, honey, lemme in," he shouts through the glass. She hates the way he calls her "honey." It makes her feel like something sticky in a jar.

Mitchell's parents are watching them from the screened porch. His father is wearing army shorts, rolled up on his bony thighs, and a white undershirt, and his mother is in red shorts and a flowered t-shirt, looking like a fat rose bush. Miranda can't get over the way she's always calm and smiling, no matter what's going on around her. Not like Miranda's mother, who was always nervous and fussy. She always wanted Miranda to clean her room, to study more and get better marks, to be a good role model to Cordelia.

When she's punished Mitchell enough, Miranda leans over and pulls up the button on his door.

"What the hell d'ya lock me out for, Randa?" Miranda sticks out her chin as if to say "let's go" and Mitchell backs out, spitting gravel in the direction of his parents.

Mitchell's house is only two miles from the south end of the beach, down a narrow road. Every time they're on it, Mitchell warns Miranda never to walk it alone. It passes through what he calls the black part of town, only he uses the n-word. He tells her she'll have nowhere to run if anyone tries anything, except into the ditch where poisonous snakes live. Miranda thinks Mitchell must be paranoid, because she's never seen a living soul in all the times they've driven this stretch. She also thinks about how much Mitchell's use of the n-word would enrage her parents, who like to think of themselves as progressive. They even attended Gay Pride parades, just to show how open they are. They used to encourage Miranda to come along. Her father said being involved in various causes would look good on her cv and make her attractive to the better universities. And her mom's work as a legal-aid lawyer made her take up many causes that she was always encouraging Miranda to care about, like fighting for refugees' rights and helping tenants battle their slum-lords.

Mitchell runs up the wooden steps of the pier in his

bare feet, his soles immune to the burning heat. Miranda follows in her flip flops. On their first day together at the beach, Mitchell had insisted on carrying her shoes, saying he'd turn her into a true Southerner yet. She'd had to jump from spot of shade to spot of shade cast onto the boards by tackle boxes sitting on the wide railing until Mitchell finally threw her back her sandals. So much for becoming a true Southerner, or a true anything. Miranda has no idea where she belongs anymore, north or south. She feels pulled in both directions, as though she's laid out on a dissecting board, pinned at either end.

They stop off at the tackle shop, where Mitchell pulls a Pepsi out of the cooler. "Hey, Rand, want anything?" he asks.

"No thanks," she calls back. Miranda is twirling the postcard rack. She hasn't written to her parents yet, but she did give her friend Shannon a note to take back to them. She'd come to Fort Lauderdale with Shannon on spring break to celebrate their final year of high school. She hadn't planned to stay; it's just the way things worked out. Her one-week trip to the beach had led her to Mitchell. Her note was short and to the point, simply stating that she'd met someone who loved her and had decided to stay. Never mind that she had only three months of high school left and had already been accepted to three different universities. She told them not to bother trying to change her mind because they wouldn't be able to. Mitchell wanted to add his two cents' worth to the note, so he'd scribbled a few lines at the bottom: *Don't worry about your daughter. She's in good hands*. The note included Mitchell's address, but no phone number. Her own cell had run out of money and she hadn't reloaded it.

Miranda can understand why they haven't called, but it perplexes her that they haven't come to take her home, forcibly, like her father once did from a party. He had pulled her right out of a slow dance with Robby Bent, who stood back amazed, and then at the last minute had called out, "Hey, don't forget to drop me your glass slipper."

"Hey, Mitch," the man behind the cash calls over.

"Hey, Bob," Mitchell calls back, tipping his Pepsi.

"Seen the picture yet?" Bob asks.

"Nope." Mitchell saunters over to the billboard near the door. His shorts are frayed, and Miranda has an urge to cut off the dangling threads.

"Hey, c'mere, Rand," he calls over.

Miranda stops twirling the postcard rack and joins him. There she is, in a five by seven colored shot, clutching a giant kingfish upside down by the tail. She's holding it at arm's length because the fish was still alive and squirming to be set free. She had caught it minutes earlier, all by herself, much to her own and everyone else's amazement.

Miranda doesn't know what to say. She can't believe that's her. It must be trick photography, the kind the tabloids are famous for, where they take two famous actors and merge them together in suggestive poses. For a second, Miranda thinks about sending the picture home to her parents. They could add it to their Miranda-book, which held pictures of all her landmarks: standing in her blue uniforms on the first day of school; sitting at a grand piano at her first music recital; middle school graduation.

Mitchell puts his arm around her and rotates her to face Bob.

"Ain't she su'um? That's the darndest looking fish I seen in a long time," he says.

"Whad'y'all do with the money?" Bob asks Miranda.

"We spent it, what d'ya think," Mitchell answers, cracking up. Miranda pats her back pocket, making sure the wad is secure. She remembers the fight they had over the hundred and fifty dollars. Mitchell wanted to spend it on better fishing gear and Miranda had a hard time not giving in. After all, she was used to people telling her what to do with her own money. She had won a graduation prize of five hundred dollars in middle school and wanted to spend it on a new bike, but her father had insisted she upgrade her computer. In the end, she'd given in. It seemed easier.

"Well, you buyin' one of those or not, girl?" Bob asks. Miranda didn't even realize that she'd begun to twirl the postcard rack again.

"Oh, sorry, I'll take this one, please." She chooses one of the beach at night — a gold sun sifting through purple clouds, black palm trees silhouetted against orange and scarlet water.

"Who's 'at for?" Mitchell asks.

"Home," she replies, not looking at him. Mitchell has told her more than once that this is now her home. She's tried to think of Fort Lauderdale that way, but can't. Home is where the heart is, they say, and her heart isn't here. It isn't anywhere, as far as she can tell. She didn't leave it behind in Toronto, except perhaps with Cordelia. Miranda's eyes are drawn to the dead starfish under Bob's glass counter. She sees her heart stuffed and laid out on display the same way, awaiting a new owner.

Down on the beach, Miranda spreads out her metal-lic blanket, a present from Mitchell. He said it would guarantee an all-round even tan, as well as a sand-free trip home. Mitchell always says anybody looking for Miranda could just follow the trail of sand she traipses into the house. Miranda pictures her parents crouched over, magnifying glasses in hand, following the sand right up Mitchell's front steps, past his parents on the porch, and into their bedroom. Progressive or not, she knows they'd be outraged to find her and Mitchell in the same bed. But where else could she stay? Her vacation money had run out. Shannon had urged her to come back, but she hadn't listened.

"You hardly know him. You can't do this. What about school?" Shannon pleaded.

"I'll be okay. Don't worry," Miranda replied. Frankly, she likes the fact that nobody in Mitchell's family gives a hoot about education. Mitchell has no career goals. He plans to fish and do odd jobs in between, if he has to. It's what all the men in his family do, apart from joining the army. Miranda knows what her parents would say about slack plans like that.

Miranda can see Mitchell way above her, setting up his tackle box. He's hoping to catch some baby sharks to sell at the Deep C Souvenir Shop. Tourists pay ten dollars to watch them float around in a large tank in the store's basement. Mitchell took Miranda a couple of weeks ago and pointed out the two he'd caught. When she asked how he could tell, he said you always recognized something you'd caught yourself. To Miranda, they all looked the same, and she only got a glimpse of their teeth once, when someone tapped the glass and they thought it meant food was coming.

Miranda doesn't want to take off her clothes right away. Her skin is burned and starting to blister under the band of her black bikini. Mitchell told her she was crazy for buying black, but she explained that she never would've bought black if she'd known she'd be staying so long.

"Hey, Ra," Mitchell calls from the pier, waving his T-shirt. The skin on his chest is red and wrinkled, like it's been deep-fried. "How come ya still got your clothes on? This is the best sun of the day."

Miranda reluctantly pulls off her T-shirt, then kicks off her shorts. She soaks her skin with sunscreen, thinking how Mitchell will tell her later that only wimps use it. "It just gyps you out of a tan." Miranda's mother once pointed out that the word *gyp* was actually an insult to gypsies, who had an unfair reputation as thieves and cheats, but there'd be absolutely no point in explaining that to Mitchell.

Miranda fixes her eyes on the waves beating insistently against the far legs of the pier, as though they're trying to topple the wooden structure. She pictures Mitchell sliding, tackle box and all, into the ocean, like a *Titanic* victim. She's not sure how she'd feel about that. She's not at all sure what her feelings for Mitchell are.

He's an alternative to going home, that's all. She hasn't agreed to marry him. Nobody she knows gets married at eighteen, but down here it's not unusual. Lots of Mitchell's friends and cousins are married already. "It's my time," he has told her. "And you're it," as though they're just playing a game of tag.

They had met at an all-night beach party that she'd gone to with Shannon. Miranda was sleeping outside, curled up in a cluster of couch grass beside some wooden steps. According to Mitchell, he spent the night sitting on the stairs, keeping watch over her. He said only southern men were gentlemen, and since most of the teenagers vacationing on the beach in March were northerners, she was lucky he was there.

In the morning, Mitchell showed her how to dig for sharks' teeth. You had to walk backwards, hunched over, digging delicately in the sand among the pebbles and bits of broken shell. She's been collecting sharks' teeth ever since and has almost a whole jar full. She takes the jar out of her straw bag and holds it up to the sun. If she turns the glass a certain way the sun glints off the black surfaces of the teeth, making them gleam. It amazes Miranda to think of all that raw power, now bottled up and harmless.

The noon sun is strong and Miranda can feel her skin bubble. She could fry an egg on her belly. She makes a visor of her hand and looks up at Mitchell, who has moved to the far end of the pier and is sitting on the middle railing, his chin resting on the top beam, as if he's stuck in a guillotine. While he's occupied, Miranda jumps up and scoops her beach gear into her straw bag, blanket and all. If Mitchell sees her he'll want to know where she's going. He doesn't like to let her out of his sight. Sometimes she can feel his eyes boring holes into her, stronger than the sun's rays.

She walks away from the pier, letting the salty water wash over her feet. When she looks back over her shoulder, she catches Mitchell hauling his rod over his head, ready to cast out. She steps backwards, landing squat in a kid's sandcastle. "Sorry," she mutters, then runs on.

Further north the beach is more crowded. The flashing sign of the arcade, the landmark that separates north from south, is just ahead. Miranda cuts through it and emerges onto Fort Lauderdale Beach Boulevard. There, she continues north, passing the bar where she danced barefoot a few months ago, dodging broken bottles.

It occurs to Miranda that if she keeps walking, she'll eventually cross into Georgia, then South and North Carolina, then Virginia, then up through Pennsylvania, New York, and finally into Canada. She could sleep on the beach down here, and maybe as far as Virginia, but no further than that. And what would her homecoming be like? Her parents must be furious. They had it all planned: her graduation, then enrolment into a Liberal Arts program. It was what they wanted her to study, because it could lead to so many interesting career paths. But Miranda's favorite subject was biology. She had a talent for it. The sight of frogs and mice waiting to be dissected never bothered her. She didn't even mind the fetal pigs that sent so many of her classmates gagging to the bathroom. Dissecting thrilled her. She couldn't wait to pin the specimen to her cutting board and explore.

Miranda keeps walking, putting more distance between herself and the busy, touristy part of town. On impulse, she turns into a motel with a large CLOSED sign in the office window. At the back, she finds an oval pool filled with green water and hundreds of dead bugs, their wings spread, floating on its surface. She stretches out in a lawn chair made of woven strips of plastic, most of them broken, and wonders if Mitchell has discovered she's gone yet. She also wonders what would happen if she pried open one of the windows and squatted inside for a while. Would Mitchell send out a search party? Would he eventually find her? And if her parents did come down, would they find Mitchell and work with him to locate her? Her parents have probably decided to make her suffer for a while before coming to get her. They probably thought this would be a good chance for her to think about her future and to practice her decision-making skills. These skills were her father's forte. He made huge decisions at work all the time and he made all the decisions around the house too, for everyone. He had even decided that Miranda shouldn't take this trip in the first place.

"You have too much school work to do. And you'll be spending all your saved money."

"But I'm almost eighteen, Dad. I'll be eighteen in a month. Legal, remember?"

"Legal? What does that mean. You're still too young to go to another country alone. Anything could happen."

She watched her father's mouth open and close as he lectured her, but tuned out the sound. She concentrated instead on her mother, who was standing behind him, her arms folded across her chest. Why didn't her mother come to her defence, like she did for all her disadvantaged clients? And hadn't she been young once too? Why couldn't she be like Shannon's mother who had just said that the trip sounded like great fun?

Miranda fixed her eyes on her tarantula paperweight. It had been a present from her mother for her fifteenth birthday. The furry spider sat in a glass bubble filled with formaldehyde, its bulging eyes watching the three of them. Miranda kept looking from the spider to her mother. She was convinced that her mother wanted her father to stop talking as much as she did, but she just didn't have the nerve to shut him up. Suddenly, Miranda picked up the paperweight — it fit into her fist like a hardball — and hurled it across the room, smashing it against the wall behind her bed.

Her father finally stopped shouting. All three of them stood and watched the glass flying off in splinters and the thick yellowish liquid oozing down the wall. Then they stared at the brown beast lying, belly-up, on her pillow.

Miranda's mother was the first to stir. She crossed the landing to the bathroom and grabbed a handful of tissue. Then she scooped up the spider, supporting the whole mess with her other hand, as if it were a baby's head. Miranda followed her back to the bathroom where the two of them stood over the toilet bowl, watching the furry creature spin around and around, until it flushed out of sight forever. Even though they didn't speak, Miranda felt it was their deepest moment of understanding ever.

Miranda left the next day while her parents were at work. She waited until they were out of the house, packed a suitcase, and went to stay at Shannon's until the flight left that evening. Her mother would have come home around five to find her gone. It would have fallen on her mother's shoulders to tell her father, who always came home later, that Miranda had disobeyed him. That wouldn't have been easy. And it couldn't be easy for her mother now, not knowing anything about Miranda's new life, except what Shannon could tell her.

Miranda walks tentatively to the edge of the pool. A rancid odor rises, released by the heat of the sun. It's not the clean water of their pool at home, so carefully filtered and purified with chlorine and other chemicals, but Miranda lifts her arms over her head and dives in anyway, separating the mass of bugs. Deep underwater, she keeps her eyes closed as her hands reach for the edge. She swims back and forth, north and south, again and again in the dirty water, coming up only when she needs air. Every time she emerges, she thinks she should stop, but a voice in her head tells her she hasn't done enough yet. She should stay in the dirty water a while longer. After so many laps, she becomes disoriented and loses track of which direction she's swimming, north or south. Which way will she be facing when she stops? A tiny voice in her head tells her it could make a difference.

Finally, when her arms and legs are dead tired, Miranda emerges, dragging herself up against the side of the pool. Ahead of her is North Fort Lauderdale Beach Boulevard stretching toward Georgia. Miranda exhales, feeling the stale air leave her body. She shakes herself off and pats as much dirty water off her skin as she can. When she combs her hair a few dead bugs stick to the teeth. She pulls her shorts and T-shirt over her wet bathing suit and grabs her straw bag. She can feel the heavy jar of sharks' teeth banging against her knee. Impulsively, she pulls it out and unscrews the lid. Then she bends down and, walking backwards, spills the black teeth in a trail that leads from the pool to the front gate. She saves only a few, to turn into earrings for Cordelia.

When she reaches the pier, Mitchell is loading his tackle gear into the Camaro.

"Hey Miranda, where ya bin?" he asks. She can tell he's annoyed.

"Nowhere, just walking."

"I caught two sharks. Wanna see them?" She doesn't really, but nods. Mitchell opens the trunk to show her two tiny sharks, no more than a foot long, lying tranquil in a cooler filled with sea water.

"I gotta go up and get the rest of my stuff. Stay here. I'll be back in a minute."

Miranda stares down at the baby sharks. As far as she knows they're too young to be separated from their mothers. For the first time in weeks Miranda can picture her own mother clearly, sitting on her antique chair in the sunporch, trying to read but putting the book down every few seconds and sighing.

She watches Mitchell walk away in his cut-off jeans and bare feet. Her parents' imaginary words are right. In twenty or thirty years Mitchell will still be doing this, fishing out a piecemeal living, hoping for souvenir sales and prize money.

She lifts the cooler, which is heavier than she thought it would be, and stumbles with it to the ocean. The foamy water rolls out to lick her toes. She wades in up to her knees. Then she tips the cooler and releases the sharks into the ocean. A voice in her head tells her that marine biology might be neat. It's something she could look into.

She walks back to Mitchell slowly. He's staring at the empty trunk, his mouth and eyes open wide, a finger scratching his sandy curls. She knows she'll never be able to explain why she did it.

She takes a deep breath and pats the prize money rolled up in her jeans pocket. Hopefully, it will cover the cost of a bus ticket home.

OUT OF
THE WOODS

Today, I'm accompanying my mom to my grand-mother's apartment. I have to do this often because my mom has agoraphobia. I look the word up in the dictionary whenever I need to remind myself that her condition is real. According to Webster's, *agora* is the ancient Greek word for market. So, technically, agora-phobia is a fear of markets. With my mom, this fear extends to all public places. I end up having to take her out a lot, as though she's the child and I'm the mother.

We take a long bus ride up the expressway that con-nects the north and south ends of the city. My mom's pretty good on this route now, but she still needs me there for support, especially when we pass the tall glass buildings in the business district. For some reason, she does better around stone and brick. I think it's the way the sky and clouds are reflected on the glass buildings' walls, like giant mirrors. I can see her shrinking, as though she's looking for a place to hide, when we pass them.

The courtyard outside my grandmother's apartment building is the most decorated one on the block; hot pink peonies hug the wall, tiger lilies sit on either side of the walkway, and wild rose bushes line the lawn along the sidewalk. Today, though, I'm convinced the janitor has gone too far when I look up to see a giant stuffed parrot tied to the trunk of a skinny birch tree near the entrance.

"Like my bird?" he asks, sitting on a lawn chair. When I was a kid he'd give me candies and my mom always made me wash the wrappers first. For her, the world is one big teeming pool of germs just waiting to invade the bodies of people she loves.

"Very nice," my mom says. I nod, trying not to laugh.

The stairwell that leads to the basement apartment is poorly lit. The damp air carries a whiff of ammonia and cigarettes, smells that will overwhelm me once we're inside. I take a deep breath and clutch the railing, careful not to let the shopping bag I'm carrying bang against the wall. In it are gifts we brought back last week from our trip to Austria.

My mom knocks lightly and I hear the familiar shuffle of my grandmother's slippers. I know she'll crack the door first, to check that we aren't strangers, before sliding the chain out of its track.

"Hi Joan, hi Kathy," my grandmother says, opening up. We step into the dark apartment. My mom is always trying to talk her brother, Doug, who lives with my grandmother, into moving upstairs to a brighter place, but he says they're happy in the cool basement. My grandmother gives us each a peck on the cheek and I watch as my mom's eyes slip down to my grandmother's chest, which is covered by a flannel housecoat.

"Did you have a nice time?" my grandmother asks as we follow her to the kitchen. The upstairs apartments have hardwood floors, but this one is tiled. *Easier to wash when Angel piddles*, my grandmother is always pointing out.

"Yes, it was nice," my mom replies. I catch her looking at the needlepoint she made my grandmother last Christmas. A log cabin sits in an evergreen forest. In the background, pointy white mountains pierce the top of the frame. Their snowy peaks have already begun to yellow from all the cigarette smoke.

We sit around the small kitchen table, which is cluttered with ashtrays, grocery store fliers, and half-finished crossword puzzles. The cupboards on the opposite wall

have so many layers of paint they don't close properly.
I know this upsets my mom. I catch her staring at the
two-inch gaps. Through them, we can see how meager
my grandmother's belongings are, like Old Mother
Hubbard's. Over the years, my mom has tried to stock
the shelves with better dishes, but these always break
or disappear. Angel's food is dumped into some bone
china, another gift from my mom, on the floor.

"So, Ma, how are you feeling?" my mom asks. This
is, after all, the real reason for our visit. To check up on
my grandmother, who had breast cancer surgery just
two weeks before we left.

"Not too bad, honey. Like that, you know?" My grandmother fills a yellow kettle and lights the gas burner,
standing a little too close. "So, what did you do in
Austria?"

"Not much, really. Mostly visited with Henry's folks,"
my mom answers. She always downplays her life around
her mother, as though she can't let on that good things
happen to her. She could tell her about the castle tour
we took or the gondola ride into the Alps. These outings
were huge accomplishments for someone with agora-
phobia. But I don't interfere. I promised myself before
we left home that I wouldn't.

My grandmother bends to light a cigarette on the
flames shooting up the sides of the kettle. She once

singed her eyelashes this way, turning them orange. Then she leans over the flame to get down the tea-tin.

"Watch your housecoat," my mom cries.

My grandmother smiles, joining us with the tea at the table.

"So, you're feeling better?" my mom asks again.

"Well, Joannie, to tell you the truth, I feel like I have a tennis ball stuck under my arm. It's more uncomfortable than sore, if you know what I mean."

But my mom doesn't know, and neither do I. How could you, unless you'd had the same operation? I did think of my grandmother while we were away. I tried to see the ornate castle through the eyes of someone who'd just lost a breast, but I couldn't. I was having too much fun skating around the grand hallways in the paper slippers that all the tourists had to wear.

"And then, too, it's so awful hot here. You feel like meat gone bad in heat like this, don't you?" My grandmother looks to me for support, but I just make a face. I can tell my mom's picturing her mother hanging from a meat hook, her skin turning mossy green.

"Are you eating all right?" my mom asks next. My grandmother nods, then stuffs a whole oatmeal cookie into her mouth, without biting first. Her cheeks puff out like a gopher's.

"How does your bedroom look?" My mom organized

the redecoration of my grandmother's room while she was in the hospital.

"Nice. Come see." We follow my grandmother down the back hall. When we pass my uncle's bedroom my grandmother says, "Angel's been so good. I hardly notice she's here." My mom tried to convince my uncle to give the dog away while my grandmother was in the hospital, but he refused. He had brought the dog home from a tavern a few weeks earlier. She's blind, so when she walks she feels the walls with her square terrier nose, leaving a trail of dog drool just above the baseboards. Plus, she was never trained and does her business on newspapers laid out along the floors.

"See?" My grandmother switches on the light, a bare bulb hanging from the ceiling. The blue paper lampshade that my mom hung up is nowhere in sight. The new, delicately flowered wallpaper that my mom talked my father into hanging is completely hidden by a clothesline strung up across the room. A few dishtowels and some socks and underwear hang from it, drip drying onto newspapers that cover the floor.

"What happened to the bed?" my mom gasps. An extra mattress has been sandwiched in between the new mattress and box-spring set.

"Well, I had nowhere to put it and I didn't want to throw it out."

"But it's your old mattress. Doug was supposed to get rid of it."

"Well, I didn't let him. I might need it one day."

"But this is too high for you," my mom says. I picture my grandmother climbing into bed at night, clutching the layers like the rungs of a ladder. Later, she'd sit high on top like the princess and the pea, looking smug.

"It's okay, honey. It's comfy, really."

The flowered bedspread my mom bought to match the wallpaper is now way too short and doesn't cover the striped material of the box spring.

I watch my mom's face fall in disappointment. I remember how excited she was when we put the final touches on the room, how much she thought her mom would love it. How she hoped it would make the room more pleasant. I have a sudden urge to rip the clothes-line down. It wouldn't be hard, just a flick of my wrist. But I don't. It wouldn't make a difference anyway. My grandmother has already left the room.

༄

I HAD TO go to the hospital with my mom the day my grandmother was booked in.

"What if we just forgot about it now? What if we just packed up and took her home?" my mom asked the doctor. "I mean, she is seventy-five. Is it really worth going through all this?" My mom said it broke her heart to see her mother in a white hospital gown with a slit exposing her down the back.

"Well, if you do that, she'll die. If we operate successfully, I see no reason why your mother won't live to be a hundred. Providing we get it all," the doctor added.

"I think Gran wants to die anyway," I said to my mom later that day in the cafeteria. The walls around us were painted bright orange, like in a fast food restaurant, probably to keep people perky. "She's always going on about how fed up she is, and she's bored to death half the time."

"That's not true," my mom said, forcing down a spoon full of pea soup.

"Yes, it is. She hates playing Bingo. That's all the old fogies in her building do. And she can't just whip downtown anymore. I think she wants to die," I repeated, biting into my ham sandwich. "The only thing she likes to do is read. And she's read every book she likes ten times over. I'd want to die too if I were her." I knew I was being cruel, but I couldn't stop myself. I get tired of tiptoeing around my mom, of being so careful about what I say, of always having to avert an anxiety attack. Sometimes, I just want to be able to open my mouth without thinking and say what's on my mind, even if I regret it later.

"She could do more if she wanted to. I'd take her downtown," my mom said weakly.

I nearly choked. How would she do that? I'd have to start carting two women around instead of just one. I pictured us holding hands like a nursery school chain on a field trip.

The day of the operation, we sat in the lounge, waiting. Even though my uncle hadn't been to work that day, the tips of his fingers were still grease-stained, his nails navy blue crescents. I didn't know much about my uncle, except that he was a mechanic and an alcoholic. And that he'd never left home. That day, for the first time, I wondered why. Was it because he'd never fallen in love? Had the years just slipped by without his noticing and one day he'd woken up to find himself forty and still living at home? What if I ended up like him? I felt myself choking as I saw myself, gray-haired and stooped over, pushing my mom around in a wheelchair, wondering what life was like on the outside.

"You know the first thing I'm gonna do for Ma, eh Joan?" my uncle said. "You know? I'm gonna bust up our old furniture. Christ, I hate that stuff." He shook his head fiercely, as if he was tossing something from it. "I'm gonna take a hammer and break it up into little pieces and throw the whole goddamn works out. It's junk. You know what I mean? Junk."

My mom nodded, not looking up. I'm sure she didn't want to be thinking about junk. She'd be thinking more along the lines of lace curtains and a nice new bedspread.

"She likes crap, though. You know what I mean? I never met anyone who likes junk as much as Ma does. Every square inch of our cupboards is taken up with crap. Our cupboards are full of boxes of old elastics and rusted paperclips. Last week I found a jar of Vaseline so old it was hard as rock, and orange."

I thought of the orderly walk-in closets my mom was for-ever rearranging in our house. Sometimes I wondered if she was adopted.

"It's taking an awful long time, don't you think?" my mom said to my dad, who sat perched on the edge of his seat, craning his neck to see outside.

"She's not the only one being operated on, you know?" my dad responded. "They're probably doing a dozen in a row."

My mom made a face. I knew she was picturing her mother and eleven other women on a conveyor belt, the doctor standing above them, slicing off breasts as they went by. It was just the type of image we had to protect my mom from, or else she'd spend weeks inside.

"I'll take it out and put it on the other side of the street in the middle of the night," my uncle continued. "Then no one'll know where it came from. You know, Henry?"

My dad was now standing at the window, staring at the opposite wing of the hospital. "Look at the nice brickwork," he said, to no one in particular. "You don't see fancy brickwork like that anymore. Now everything's slapped together, like that." He clapped his hands like he was throwing together a salami sandwich.

"That's right. That's how that furniture is made. I bet I could tear it apart with my own hands," my uncle jumped in.

I fixed my eyes on a sign — *Surgery Bay*. What an odd name! I pictured the operation taking place in a large murky pond, my grandmother floating on some giant lily pad, the sound of croaking filling the air around her. I had to shut out the voices around me, and all the talk of how things were put together and torn apart. I was hearing it through my mom's ears and by the terror-stricken look on her face, I knew her anxiety was mounting.

I got up, feeling, as I always do, that I shouldn't leave my mom's side. When I passed the nurses' station, I overheard two nurses talking about Florida.

"We went to the Everglades. Man, you should've seen the alligators. Tom wanted to stop the car and get out. I said no bloody way. I could just see my leg getting chomped off." She raised a white-nyloned leg and the other nurse laughed.

It occurred to me that I too was a nurse, only I hadn't had any formal training. I had learned by experience, beginning at the age of four, holding my mom's hand when we went downtown. Even then I could tell that she was the one doing the holding and that my small hand was her anchor. Once, at a large department store, she had to go to the bathroom. I waited outside her stall, trying to see the traffic through the open window. It was taking her a long time. Eventually, I called her name, but she didn't answer. I tried to open her door but couldn't. I left and wandered in and out of the racks of clothes until I found a saleslady. I pointed to the bathroom and gestured. When we got there, my mom was splashing water on her face at one of the sinks. She shrieked when she saw me with the strange woman and pulled me to her side, like I'd been kidnapped. It never occurred to her that she was the one who had abandoned me.

The buzzer sounded and the nurses rolled their eyes. "Probably Mrs. Benezra wanting to pee again," one of them said.

I turned back to the lounge.

ᔐ

THE DAY AFTER the operation, my mom wanted to stop to buy an African Violet at the gift shop. "It'll be dead in a week," I said, but she didn't believe me, so I headed up to my grandmother's room alone. I told myself my mother would be fine navigating the elevator up to the seventh floor without me. Besides, she could text me if she needed help and I'd come down to get her.

My grandmother was lying on her side, the sheet pulled up to her chin. Her face was puffy, like it had been blown up. A plastic tube connected to a container filled with two red balls drew my attention on her bedside table. I picked it up and blew into it, sending the balls floating up to the top.

"What's this, Gran?" I asked.

"A lung exerciser, sweetie. I'm supposed to blow into it once an hour. Kathy … have you seen Doug?"

"Yes," I lied. "He's here somewhere." I actually hadn't seen him since yesterday, but knew she'd be frantic if I told her so.

My grandmother closed her eyes and fell asleep. When my mom walked into the room, I was blowing into the lung exerciser. She gasped and called out, "Kathy, put that thing down. How can you touch it?" I knew she was picturing it being passed around the cancer ward, collecting more and more deadly germs as sick people blew into it.

"It's not gonna kill me, Mom."

"Did she wake up yet?"

"Uh-huh."

"Well, what did she say?"

"Nothing. She just said hello."

"Did she ask to see me?"

"I told her you were on your way up," I lied again.

"Are you sure she heard you?"

"Well, I guess she did. She nodded, then fell asleep."

My mom looked at the floor, dejected.

⌇

LATER THAT AFTERNOON, my grandmother was sitting up in bed. The blinds were sealed tight, shutting out the sunlight.

"How are you feeling?" my mom asked, squeezing her mother's hand.

"Well, like that, I guess." There were splotches of dried blood on her neck. A clear plastic tube came out from behind her waist, dark red clumps of blood from her wound draining into it.

"You should ask the nurse to open your blinds a little," my mom said. The African Violet sat on the sill, its lilac flowers already a little withered. My grandmother just shrugged.

Then my uncle showed up. I could smell the alcohol on his breath.

"Hey, little one," he said to his mother. "How's it going?"

"Okay, my honey," my grandmother answered, brightening.

"Doug, promise me you'll let Joan take you home, eh? No going out tonight, promise me."

"She's such a little worrier," my uncle said to us in a childish voice, as though his mother were a cute little poodle. "Yeah, yeah, don't worry. I'll go home with Joannie. I'll just go get a coffee, okay, little one?" He began filling his pipe with tobacco as he walked out. I knew we wouldn't see him again today.

"Do you like the flowers, Ma?" my mom asked softly.

"Yeah, they're pretty, Joan," my grandmother said without looking at them, her voice heavy and distracted. She looked up at my mom. "You'll take Doug home, won't you, Joan?"

My mom nodded, as if taking him home were really a possibility. Did my grandmother think we had come by car? Did she even know that my mom couldn't drive anymore? That I had brought her to the hospital on three connecting buses because she couldn't take the metro either? That with each bus my mom had grown more reluctant, her weight increasing against me, as though she were collapsing?

"So?" my mom asked. I knew she wanted to bring

up the operation. My grandmother hadn't asked us about it yet. I knew my mom was dying to reassure her, to tell her that the doctor had said everything was going to be fine.

"Please, Joan, go and find him," my grandmother said finally. She turned her head so quickly that the draining tube puckered, sticking up like a V beside her chest. My mom sighed. I hoped she wouldn't try to flatten it herself.

"Come on, let's go Mom," I called firmly. "There's no point in staying." I pulled her arm up and she rose with it, completely pliable. At the door, we turned back to look at my grandmother, whose eyes were already closed.

∽

SHE'S NOT OUT of the woods yet," was an expression my mom used a lot the following week. She used it the day I brought cards to the hospital to play gin rummy with my grandmother. She used it the day my uncle brought up a CD player so she could listen to her favorite Irish and Scottish folk songs. And she said it when my dad reminded her that we had plane tickets to Austria in a week, tickets that had been purchased long before my grandmother had even discovered the lump.

"It's just that I can't leave her now, you know?"

"No, I don't know. There's nothing more you can do for her. You did your duty. Christ, you've been at the hospital every single day. She'll be home soon. We're going, now come on."

My dad often pretended my mom was not agora-phobic. It was his way of coping.

The next day my mom and I went to Walmart, where she bought a puffy blouse in the maternity section for my grandmother to wear home. The first thing we showed her was her new room, which my mom had made my dad work on every evening the previous week.

Later, when my grandmother was settled in her new bed, my mom broke the news about our trip.

"Well, I guess we're going to Austria to visit Henry's family. Henry wants to see his brother, it's been a while, and he wants us to go with him this time." She said it all quickly, as though she had rehearsed the speech several times.

My grandmother didn't say a word. She merely lit a cigarette.

"But, if you don't think you'll be all right, we won't go." I could feel her hoping her mother would ask her to stay.

My grandmother merely puffed up her blouse to make both sides even. "Oh no, dear, don't be silly. I have Doug."

I watched my mom's face fall, and for the first time in a long time I wished I knew how to pick it up again.

∽

AFTER THE TOUR of the new room, the three of us sit back down at the kitchen table. The front door bangs shut and a few seconds later my uncle walks into the room. As usual, the smell of alcohol wafts around him, inches thick.

"Hi ya, Joannie. Hi Kathy. Did you have a nice trip?"

"Yeah, it was nice," my mom says.

"That's good. And you, little one, are you okay?" he asks my grandmother, patting her head.

"Okay, Dougie," she says.

"Where's my little Angel?" My uncle disappears down the hall and reappears a minute later with the dog at his heels. Angel heads straight to where my mom is sitting, nudging her snout along her leg. My mom pushes her chair back, but the dog just edges forward.

My uncle pulls the tab off a can of beer. "Want one, Joan?"

"No thanks."

"So, Ma's looking good, eh?"

I watch my mom concentrate on her mother's face. I'm sure she's noticing the deep dark circles under her eyes and her blotchy skin. But she just nods in agreement.

"Hey, want to see something neat some guy off the ships gave me today?" My uncle holds up a brown clump that looks like gnarled fingers. "It's ginger, real ginger. Ever seen real ginger before?" He shoves it in my mom's face. She scrunches her nose and pulls back.

"It comes from a long ways away. All the way from the Caribbean. Can you imagine ever going that far?" he asks, as if he's forgotten that we've just returned from Europe. I recall my mom's face on the plane as she looked out the window at the bed of clouds that seemed to be keeping us afloat. She looked light and free, all her worry lines lifted. Nobody on the plane would have guessed she was ill.

My uncle teases his mother, waving the clump of ginger up and down like a ship on the waves.

"Never mind," my grandmother says. "I went far enough away. I felt like I was in outer space under those big machines at the hospital."

I picture the gifts waiting in the shopping bag, the ceramic plaque of the Schönbrunn Castle, the linen wall-hanging of the Danube, and the mug with an etching of the Alps on its front, things that will just end up in some cupboard, forgotten. "We went to a beautiful castle," I say, for my mom's sake. "And took a gondola up the Alps." I can feel her withdrawing, closing off, shrinking the borders around herself.

"Yeah, that's good, but this is real ginger. Not the cheap stuff you get all ground up." My uncle is so excited he misses his mouth and the beer dribbles down his chin.

Just then, Angel jumps up and paws at my grandmother's chest, pulling open her housecoat. My mom
gasps as my grandmother springs up, batting ineffectu-
ally at the blind dog. Between the loose lapels of her
housecoat the dark red arch of the cut is now exposed.
If my grandmother leaned forward we'd see it plunge
even farther into her chest. My mom is staring at the
wound, her hand over her mouth, as if she's stifling
a scream.

My uncle giggles and my grandmother is smiling
as she closes her housecoat.

It suddenly occurs to me that my mom's entire life
must have been like this — my grandmother and uncle
amusing themselves with Mom's sensitivity, my mom
cringing beside them.

"We have to go," I say decisively, jumping up. I can't
let it keep happening. I have to rescue her or she'll get
worse and I'll be stuck chaperoning her forever. I push
past my uncle and hold out my hand to my mom. She
grabs it like a life saver and I pull her up.

"These are for you," I snap, throwing the bag of gifts
to the floor, hoping the plaque and mug will smash
and that Angel's pee, which is already spreading under
the bag, will soak the wall hanging.

"You sure, Joannie?" my uncle asks, looping his
finger under Angel's collar. He seems disappointed, as

though he was just warming up and is now going to miss the real fun.

"Take care, honey," my grandmother says, reaching up on tippy toes to kiss my mom.

When she turns to me I pull away. Our eyes lock and I send her a cold look. I need her to see that I see her cruelty, even if she doesn't. I stare until I feel I'm cutting her down, diminishing her until she's nothing but a scar in the corner of my mind.

We walk past the gaudy parrot tied like a prisoner to the tree in the courtyard. If it could speak, what would it say? Would it repeat the same words over and over again, or would it learn some new ones every now and then?

My mom's staring at the bird as well. I pull her hand and lead her on. A voice in my head keeps saying, we're definitely not out of the woods yet.

ICE

When I'm near him he turns to stone. He stands there, immobile, his face turned away from me, as if the sight of me would kill him. I know I should go away and put him out of his misery, but it's hard to stay out of your own father's way when you're the only two people living together in a small, two-bedroom apartment.

A typical scenario goes like this: he's standing in the tiny kitchen looking for something in the drawers, pulling them open one at a time then slamming them closed. I tip-toe into the room, trying to be quiet. When he hears me behind him he freezes, a drawer open at the end of his arm. He stares inside, at the messy heap of knives, elastics and plastic popsicle sticks that nobody ever bothers to use any more, as though he wishes he could crawl inside and shut the drawer behind him.

Sometimes, I try to start a conversation. I'll say something simple like *good morning*. He might groan or nod, but that's all. He never asks me how I'm doing or what's happening at school. I think I could say anything and get the same non-response. I could say, *Hey Dad, I tried heroin last night*, or *Hey Dad, I'm pregnant*. It's not what I'm saying; it's the fact that I'm there, so near to him, that's the problem.

Sometimes, he'll look as though he wants to speak to me. His face will soften, then hesitate, then harden again. I can actually feel him shaking me out of his head, like some useless words that suddenly have no meaning.

Of course, it wasn't always like this. When I was really young, before I had even started school, we did some neat things together. My mom worked downtown and my dad worked from home, so we were together a lot. My favorite memory is of the two of us sitting in the beat up vw van outside my brother's school. We'd put on fake noses attached to plastic glasses and old wigs that my mother found at garage sales. We called it spying on my brother. When we saw him in the school-yard we ducked below the dash or behind the steering wheel, giggling.

It never occurred to me then that the orange van, with its lime green and yellow peace symbols, was a dead giveaway.

✍

YESTERDAY, I WAS at my best friend Nikki's house when Tim called her to talk about me. He didn't know I was there, listening in on the speaker phone.

"I really like Cal, I mean I *really* like her, but she's so cool with me."

I had to put a pillow over my mouth to stop him from hearing me gag. I don't mind Tim. He's okay. He's kind of cute really. He has blond hair that he wears long and cut square around his face, as if he doesn't realize the Beatles went out of style decades ago. He's always blushing when I'm around.

"Do you think she'd go out with me?"

"Umm, I don't know. She might," Nikki responded, trying to pull the pillow off me.

There was a long silence, and then, out of the blue, in a voice I'd never heard Tim use before, he shouted into the phone, "I bet that bitch wouldn't. She's so cold and aloof, it's like she's made of ice. She never goes out of her way for me. Like it would kill her to give me the time of day." Then the line went dead and I pictured him throwing down his phone so hard it sank to the center of the earth, all the way to China, where my brother and I used to try to dig to at the beach.

I was stunned. There was more than anger in Tim's voice. There was hatred, real hatred.

Nikki didn't speak to me right away, as if she knew I'd be embarrassed.

I was suddenly so cold I was shivering, even though it must have been a hundred degrees in Nikki's basement. It was like someone had doused me with ice water.

∽

WALKING HOME, I passed by the family with the disabled daughter. The father was standing on the porch, his head down, staring at his shoes. The mother was in the yard, trying to coax the girl out from behind the huge fir tree, a beach bag with rolled up towels looped over her arm. I could see the daughter's head poking through the branches. She was laughing like a kid in the middle of a game of hide-and-seek, but her father wasn't amused. His shoulders were slumped, as though he carried the weight of many hard years on them. I recognized the expression of shame that covered his face. Every time the mother called, "Come on out Carol, right now, or we won't go swimming," he winced.

I tried to smile at the father. I wanted to show him that he didn't have to feel the way he did. It wasn't his fault that his daughter was the way she was. It wasn't her fault either. It wasn't anyone's fault. I pictured him running down into the yard and indulging his daughter, who was still squealing with delight as her mother tried to lure her out from behind the tree. Maybe if they pretended it was a game, they could corner her, the way my mother and father used to corner me and my brother around the kitchen table.

It occurs to me now that my feelings about the struggling family are proof that I'm not aloof. I just come across that way. It's my way of protecting myself from the outside world. Everyone has their own way of doing this. Nikki's defense is to expand herself. She sprawls over everything, taking up twice as much space as she should for such a tiny person. I've often watched the way she'll automatically grab two chairs, one for her torso and one for the overflow of legs, arms, bags, or rackets that she spreads around herself like tentacles. I guess it's her way of saying, "I'm here. Just because I'm small doesn't mean you can ignore me."

At home, I'm the opposite of Nikki. I'm always trying to take up less and less space, to curl myself up like a hermit crab. I have the smallest bedroom, even though my father offered me the big one when we first moved here after the accident.

"Take it, go on, girls need room, you'll want your

space," he coaxed. That was when he could still look me in the eyes.

"No, no, it's okay. You take it," I responded. The huge empty room made me feel like the breath had been punched out of me. The space was too vast. The polished hardwood planks looked like giant bridges that I'd be afraid to cross.

"I want the small room, Dad, really." He didn't persist, and I squeezed my stuff — single bed, desk, bookshelf, blow-up chair — into the tiny room at the end of the hall. When Nikki's over she sprawls so badly I hardly have any space for myself.

৵

THIS MORNING, I'M curled up on my bed going over Tim's words. I'm remembering things that seemed innocent at the time: Tim pushing his way into the circle at recess and me pretty much ignoring him, Tim's party where Nikki drank too much beer and spent the night buzzing around on top of the furniture like a bee. It was Tim who calmed her with orange juice and helped me walk her home. At the door to Nikki's house I simply spat, *You know you shouldn't let people drink so much*, and then slammed the door in his face. Tim's eyes were always on me in class, like he was trying to inflict some kind of voodoo spell. I always shook him off by rolling my eyes past his face.

I decide I need a plan of action, so I call Nikki.

"Hey, is anyone going to the dance at City?" City is a community college at the tip of the island. They hold dances, which we call beer bashes, on a regular basis and we can usually get in even if we don't have college I.D.S.

"Yeah, I think everyone's going. Why? You want to go?"

"Do you think Tim's going?"

"Ah-ha! Now I get it. You want to get back at him, right?"

"Something like that." But she couldn't be more wrong. I don't want revenge. Revenge is for when you're wronged. But I don't feel wronged. I feel found out, exposed. I picture Tim telling everyone what he thinks of me, the whole gang suddenly looking at me like a cold, hard bitch. But the truth is that I want Tim to like me. His attention has been so constant. He's been like a thought that tickles the corner of my brain, or a piece of hair that hangs in my line of vision, creating a blur that can't be blown away. I want Tim to keep looking at me with that expression, that puppy dog look of adoration that I've taken for granted all year.

But then I hear the abrupt silence of Tim's phone and the image of his gentle expression disappears.

I pick up the photograph of my brother, taken when

he was in grade eleven, only months before his death. I run my finger over the glass, picking up a trail of dust. He was four years older than me, old enough to have looked after me when I was little. He never seemed to mind dragging me along to the park, to the pool. His patience was infinite. If he were still alive, he'd be twenty. I wonder if he'd still be my protector, if I could have gone to him and told him how I was afraid to be soft, to let Tim or anyone else in.

But then, I remind myself, my hard shell only formed the minute those two police officers entered the hall of our old house.

"Good evening, Sir," they said to my father. "Are you the father of Nathan Cole? And the husband of Emily?"

My father's knees buckled. My mother had taken Nathan to a swim meet across the Ontario border in Cornwall. Nathan had just gotten his driver's license and he'd been begging my mother to let him drive. My father had given my mother an encouraging wink, to let her know that he approved. He used to let us steer the old vw van when we were little. He'd let go at the top of our street and call over to whoever was lucky enough to be sitting in the passenger seat, *Okay, kid, take over. Keep her steady.* My mother's last words to Nathan before leaving home had been, *We'll see.*

We later learned that Nathan had been driving when

an eighteen-wheeler spun out of control on some black ice on the other side of the 401 and skidded across the median to hit them head on. Our car was found upside down in the ditch. That's how the memory of my mother and brother is fixed in my mind: the two of them dangling like upside-down puppets above the dashboard.

That night, the patch of black ice that streaked across the highway slipped inside me and coated my bones.

Nathan, I say to the picture, *if you're out there, please help me melt. Help some of what you were rub off on me.* Nathan was warm, funny, and affectionate. He never passed me without ruffling up my hair or pinching my cheek or play punching me in the arm. He hugged me and adored me and I never ever felt afraid of anything when Nathan was alive.

～

"WHERE ARE YOU going?" my father asks as I walk past him to grab my jean jacket out of the closet. It's so rare that he questions me I jump a little.

"Out with Nikki."

"Out where with Nikki?"

"I don't know yet, just around."

My father stares in a way that makes me want to crawl into the closet and shut the door. I can't let him in, not now.

Then he surprises me by saying, "Well, be careful," rather sweetly.

"I will. See ya."

Nikki's mother drives us out to City College, reminding us the whole way there that no matter how late it is when we leave we are not to take a lift from anyone who's been drinking. We are to call her and she'll come right away, even if we tear her out of a sound sleep. Nikki's mother and my mother were friends. I think she now feels obliged to shelter me a little.

"We will, we will," we both promise.

In the back seat, Nikki whispers in my ear that Tim is definitely going to be there. She actually called him to find out.

"Did he ask if I'm going?"

"No, but he'll know you're going if I'm going," Nikki says to encourage me.

Nikki's mother reminds us once again of our promise to call her and then tells us to have a good time. I wonder if she knows what really goes on at these "dances." She probably figures that, because they're on a college campus, they're safe. I'm sure she has no idea that you can buy weed and more in the washroom, and that security is two old guys who sit playing cards at a fold-out table, well away from the action.

Nobody asks to see I.D. and we walk in easily and find our gang. People have already begun to pile empty plastic beer mugs into a pyramid. I sit next to Tim, but he doesn't look at me. Last time we were at a City beer bash together he spent the whole night fetching drinks for me and Nikki. We were supposed to ride home with him but we ducked into the washroom to hide, just for a joke. We giggled until we almost peed our pants picturing him looking for us. He kept texting us but we just ignored our phones. When we came out he was gone and we had to call Nikki's mother.

Tim is drinking more than usual. He usually nurses a beer all evening because he's the one who drives a bunch of people home in his Jeep. I've always loved to watch Tim drive. He seems to meld into the machine, his hands and feet working the pedals and gears grace-fully, like a choreographed dance.

"Hey Tim, how many have you had?" I try to say lightly, tugging his sleeve. He shrugs.

"Dunno. What's it to you?"

Nikki comes back with a beer for each of us.

"Well, cheers," I say to Tim, knocking my plastic mug against his. He looks a bit stunned, like this may be a trick.

I carry on like that, trying to pay him attention when normally I wouldn't. The music is so loud it's impossible to talk. I have to communicate through gestures and expressions. But I can feel him softening a bit. I mimic dancing with my fingers on the table to ask if he wants to. He shrugs in response and we both get up.

We dance one fast tune. It's a college cover band that's playing top ten kind of stuff, some rock, some pop, even a little bad rap. At the end of this number the tempo changes to slow and Tim actually holds out his arms to me. I step into them. He's stocky and I like the feeling of being little and wrapped up inside him. His breath is on my neck and his hand is drawing gentle circles on my back.

But when the song ends Tim just lets go and walks back to the table where he downs another beer. Nikki looks at us, confused. I'm sure she's wondering when my delicious moment of revenge will strike. The pyramid on the table is getting higher. Some of the cups still have a bit of beer in them and they sway precariously.

Next thing I know, Tim is pulling Nikki up, coaxing her onto the dance floor. She looks back over her shoulder at me and shrugs as she follows him. I decide to go to the bathroom. When I come back they're still dancing. I can barely see them tucked way into the middle of the dance floor, thumping away in the crowd to a heavy metal number. I'm completely alone at the table.

An image of my father, his face hardened by pain, flashes in my mind. I see him turning away, acting as though he has nothing to give me. I'm just a sixteen-year-old girl that he has no idea how to reach. He has no idea what I might need. Like the time I got my first period. He knew and I knew he knew because of the rolled up pads in the bathroom garbage which he would empty at night, as if to hide the evidence. He was going to leave all that to my mother, but she was gone. My reverie is interrupted by the huge crash of a table collapsing in the dark. Nikki is weaving her way back through the crowd.

"Hey," she says. "Everyone's up there. Why don't you come?"

I know she's right. If I don't force myself to join in, I'll be sitting on the outside forever. I need to find Tim and make him like me again. But when we get back to the dance floor, he's dancing with some girl I don't know. He seems so into the music, his eyes closed, his square hair banging against his face. I take a deep breath and move right up beside him. I'll do whatever it takes. I'll be attentive, I won't turn away. I'll be soft and sweet, and yield completely. If only Tim will open his eyes and fix me with that adoring look.

Suddenly, I remember when I was twelve and wanted to show my father that I could do a perfect dive. I wanted to show him how gracefully I could spring off the edge and slice into the water, like a dolphin. I was so anxious, I ran and dived in too soon, too close to the shallow end, and scraped my nose along the bottom. I didn't want to emerge, for him to see the red streak along my nose that proved I had screwed up. But when I came up he had already turned to go home. I never did know if he saw me. It was the summer after the accident and he had already started to drift away.

I'm diving into the pool again now, beside Tim. I dance as though I really mean it, to make it clear to this other girl that Tim's with me. Eventually she twirls away, not seeming to care. I tug on Tim's sleeve to get his attention. He opens his eyes and looks down at me, a slight flash of recognition in his eyes. Then he's gone again, bending and twisting to the beat of an old Rolling Stones hit, oblivious to everything. Or so I think, until he suddenly pulls me against him. He dances me around, leaning heavily on me. It's obvious he's drank way more than he's used to. He keeps pulling me close then pushing me back, sometimes hard enough that I feel my ribs slamming into his. The music changes tempo and Tim and I just keep doing this weird dance around and around. If he's looking at me at all it's between half-closed eyes.

Finally, the band stops playing and announces a

short break. Our bodies stop moving and readjust slowly to the pull of gravity. Tim is finally looking at me.

"Can I take you home?" he asks.

"Sure," I say, hoping it's just the two of us in the Jeep. It'll give me a chance to make a gesture.

We walk back to the table holding hands. Nikki is there, watching us. She raises her shoulder slightly, to ask me what's up.

"I'm taking a lift with Tim," I tell her. I know I'm breaking our unwritten rule about never leaving without the other, but I hope she'll forgive me.

"Okay," Nikki says tentatively. She probably still thinks I'm up to something and have plans to dump Tim in the parking lot. She winks as if to encourage me and calls out, "See you guys later" as she heads to the bathroom.

Tim is finishing his last beer. I can't tell how many he's had. I hear Nikki's mother making us promise to call her, but I can't back out now. The anger in Tim's voice over the phone is still fresh and cutting in my mind.

Tim stands abruptly, stumbling into the table. He reaches up, swaying, and places his plastic mug on the peak of the wobbling pyramid. Before I can back away, the whole structure collapses. The mugs tumble, dousing me with a shower of warm beer.

"Shit," says Tim.

I almost scream something nasty, but don't. "Never mind. Come on, let's go." I pull him along, trying to ignore the voice in my head that's telling me it's not safe to go home with him.

Once in the Jeep, Tim seems to sober up. At least, he has no trouble fitting the key in the ignition and working the complex system of pedals and sticks to back us out of the parking lot. He still hasn't really acknowledged me, not in the way I want him to. But there's time. It's a half hour drive and I don't have a curfew. We could stop somewhere. My father doesn't even notice what time I come home anymore.

"Let's take the scenic route," Tim calls across to me. The tarp isn't up and the night wind pulls his voice away.

"Sure, I guess." The scenic route means taking the winding road along the lake instead of the highway. I remind myself of all the times Tim has driven me and Nikki safely home.

We wind along, not speaking, twisting down toward the lake. I know that Tim's silence is my fault. I've rebuked him too many times. If he were driving someone else, he'd be more chatty. He'd be laughing across the stick shift, making gestures with his free hand.

Tim takes an abrupt right turn onto a dark wooded road. It goes by fast, so I can't be sure, but I think I saw a *No Entry/Wrong Way* sign at the corner. I must be wrong.

Tim would have seen it for sure. He must know this as a short cut down to the lake. If I question him, he'll think I don't trust him and it will make things worse.

My breath catches. In the distance, I see headlights approaching. What if this really is a one-way street? Will the oncoming vehicle see our lights and stop? Or will Tim see the white lights and figure it out?

My father's face flashes in my mind, again. I see him shrug and walk away. I see his head hung low. I see the way he feels he can't help me. And in that instant, with the opposing headlights looming so close I think I can feel their heat, I understand my father's shame. He isn't ashamed of me, but of himself, of his inadequacy. How can he be father and mother to me all at once? And how can he take the place of Nathan?

I am Nathan in the front seat, staring helplessly at the approaching headlights, unable to maneuver around them. My mother is beside me, frozen in terror. Our hands reach for one another as the brakes screech. I see my father, receiving the news of my death from the local police. He crashes and falls to the ground. I hear him scream. It hits me, like the full force of a truck, that I am all he has.

"Tim, you idiot! You're going the wrong way! You're going to get us killed!" I yell, forgetting all my resolutions about being nice.

Tim jumps on the brakes and steers the Jeep to the right, sliding us to an almost graceful stop by the side of the road.

"You could have killed us! You shouldn't be driving — you know you shouldn't. What the hell are you trying to prove?" I keep yelling, unable to stop. I know I promised to be soft and sweet, but the words won't stop coming. It's as though my anger is out of control, careening across the frozen space between us and ramming into him.

Tim's head is down on the steering wheel. He pulls it up slowly. He looks shaken, tears starting to form in the corners of his eyes.

"God, Cal, I'm so sorry," he says. "I just wanted to be alone with you somehow, to show you ..." His words break off and I brace myself, waiting for him to turn on me, to yell at me the way he did on the phone, as if it's my fault that he's so messed up, as if it's my fault he couldn't see the sign at the top of the road. I see my father again, his characteristic shrug of the shoulder, his helplessness at not being able to undo the tragedy on that other dark road.

But then it happens. Tim looks at me the old way, his soft blue eyes gazing at me from under his bangs. He looks at me the way I crave, the way I'm afraid I'll never stop craving.

"Cal, I feel so stupid."

I know that he's calling on me to help him, to give him a little something. He is calling on me to tell him it's all right. I reach across and push the thick bangs away from his face, gently.

"It's okay, Tim. It was an accident. Forget it. It wasn't your fault. It wasn't anyone's fault." I know I'm talking about tonight, but I'm also talking about something else, something way beyond this moment. Something that has to do with connections and how tender they can be and how deep the hurt can cut when they're broken.

"Let's get out and walk around. You'll feel better. You shouldn't be driving you know?"

"Yeah, I know. Pretty dumb, huh?"

Yeah, pretty dumb, I think. But I don't say it. I'm just as dumb for taking the lift. I hop out and run around to the other side to help Tim out of the Jeep. Then we hook hands and look around. In the distance, moonlight is stretched out on the surface of the lake, like a long white arm. It's the only light on the otherwise dark road. Without any hesitation, we turn and head towards it.

MY COUSIN
JACK

Today is the day of my cousin Jack's home-coming. My mother and I have come over early, to help my aunt decorate her house, which is the top floor of an old duplex We've laced the hallway with twisted crepe paper, dotted the living room walls with balloons — rubbed on our hair for stick — and hung a green banner that says "Welcome Home" over the entryway. This whole fuss seems totally wrong to me, as if Jack is a soldier returning from war, with purple hearts hanging off his chest.

The truth is that Jack is coming home from the mental hospital where he has spent the last four months recovering from a nervous breakdown.

"Jody," my mother calls from the kitchen. When I get

there, she points to three bowls sitting on the counter. In them are chips, Cheezies, and pretzels. Suddenly, I can't hold my tongue. "Isn't this a bit much? I mean, this isn't really a party, is it?"

"Just spread these around the front room. Please." Her last word is a plea.

"Okay, but Jack's going to hate all this fuss."

My mother shoots me an angry look, covers her lips with an index finger, and points in the direction of my aunt's bedroom. She's in there getting ready, probably dressing way up in some party dress. I suddenly understand who all this fuss is for. It's necessary camouflage, to help my aunt forget where Jack has been and why.

I place the bowls as gingerly as I can between all the porcelain ballerinas that decorate my aunt's living-room. Between two swans a picture of Jack sits in a gold frame. It's Jack as I remember him, with gentle brown eyes and a warm smile. It's hard to imagine this face going through what Jack's been through in the last few months. It's hard to imagine it bruised or bloated from the drugs they gave him in the hospital.

There's nothing to do now but sit and wait. Wait and speculate. What will Jack look like? What will he say? What will he be like? Will he still be my Jack, the kind and gentle kid I was best friends with until we moved away from Verdun last July, almost a year ago?

My father finally shows up. "So?" he says sarcastically. "Where are they?" He says "they" with scorn, like my mother and aunt deserve his anger. My father has no patience for this entire affair. According to him, Jack's downfall was inevitable. He asked for it by being too soft. My father grew up on military bases because his father was in the army. He spent a lot of time telling Jack he had to be less sensitive, to grow a thicker skin. He said he knew this downfall would come if Jack didn't toughen up. "Besides," he once said. "People get attacked every day. Most of them just pick themselves up and get on with it."

My father has spent the year trying to convince me to forget about Jack. He reminds me, whenever he can, that Jack isn't really my cousin and his mom isn't really my aunt. I only call her that because she and my mother have been best friends forever. I sometimes think that my father moved us to the suburbs to separate me and Jack.

As if the new neighborhood could wipe out sixteen years of friendship.

∽

I WAS AT my boyfriend Dutchie's house watching him and his friends play pool when my mother called to tell me that Jack had been attacked. The ringtone of my phone made Dutchie lose his concentration and he fanned, sending the white ball into the middle of the green, nowhere near anything.

"What happened?" I asked, but she wouldn't tell me. She just kept repeating that Jack had been attacked. Then she said, her voice squeaking, "Come home right away," as if I was in danger too.

Dutchie said I was as white as the cue ball when I hung up.

I walked home, down the streets of the new neighborhood that were still strange to me. They were wide and quiet, with tall hedges separating the houses, so that all you could see were the roofs. A gray driveway rolled out beside each one like a tongue. I shuddered as I passed Diane's house, certain that she must be smirking down at me. I guess she was the closest thing to a friend I had here, although "friend" sometimes seemed like the wrong word. Halloween night, she'd told me not to bother buying candies. "Nobody will ring your bell," she said. "They don't know you yet." As if we might slip razor blades into apples or dip candies in poison.

When I got home all the lights in our townhouse were off and the blinds were drawn.

"Why's it so dark?" I called out.

"Sssh! Come in and close the door," my mother whispered. She'd been acting strangely ever since our move away from Verdun, the beloved neighborhood we'd both grown up in. The day of the actual move, my father practically had to drag her into the high cab of the truck he'd rented. All year I've been expecting her to migrate back there, like a lost cat. She still can't get used to having a backyard and sits on the back steps to smoke, as if the grass might be a mine field. And without corner stores to walk to we are constantly running out of things like milk and bread. My father drives her to the supermarket every Saturday and urges her to do a big order. *Get it all in, for the whole week*, he'll say. But she can't. She's never piled an entire shopping cart with food in her life.

My father came home right after me. I guess she'd called him too. Both of us sat anchored to the sofa while my mother paced above us in the dark.

"Well?" my father asked, swinging his leg. When he threatened to turn the light on, my mother pushed him back down and blurted out the story of how Jack had been attacked and left bleeding on one of the little bridges that span the aqueduct near his house. Whoever had done it spray-painted the word "fag" on the railing beside him. Jack was now in the hospital.

"He has several broken ribs and his face is smashed. He might lose an eye. He's barely conscious and he may have frostbite on top of everything else." My mother was sobbing. I didn't know what to say. I imagined Jack all purple against the white hospital pillow. I felt as though I'd been punched myself, especially when I thought about how poorly I'd stayed in touch with Jack since our move.

"Why are you so upset?" my father eventually asked when my mother wouldn't stop crying. "Jack's not our son." I didn't know how my father could be so callous. He's always resented the closeness of our two families, possibly because he's the odd man out. My aunt's husband died when Jack was little. That left no one for my father to pair off with when we got together. I tuned him out by picturing the word "fag." Did they do it graffiti style, with round or triangular letters, or did they just spray paint it fast and careless to get away faster?

Then I thought about its meaning. Fag — gay — homosexual. It's what some kids used to call Jack, just because he was quiet and mild-mannered. When we'd fish in the river, Jack would sit too far back and barely skim the water's surface with his hook. Once, he saved a kitten that some kids had tried to drown in a plastic bag weighted with rocks. Afterwards, he cradled the petrified kitten in his arms until it stopped shaking. Jack loved animals. He wanted to be a vet. But that didn't mean he was gay.

And, even if he was, that was no reason to beat him to a pulp.

That night I cried, burying my face deep in my pillow to muffle the sound. I whispered to Jack, hoping he'd hear me, that we were still connected, like we used to be. *I'm sorry, Jack. I've been a shitty friend. I just didn't know how to get back there from here, to fit in here and still be with you. And then I met Dutchie.*

Could I really explain Dutchie to Jack? Could I tell him that ever since I'd started going out with Dutchie, I had begun to feel grounded? That before that, the new neighborhood was like a foreign country and I was desperate to learn its rules and customs. In Verdun, the boundaries were visible, the St. Lawrence River to the south, the aqueduct to the north, the Wellington Tunnel to the east. But here in Dollard, a big beige suburb with hardly any trees and no water, the boundaries were invisible. Sure, there was the Trans-Canada Highway to the south and another suburb farther north, but they didn't mean a thing. The boundaries that I kept trying to figure out were the intangible ones, the codes of dress and behavior that I was constantly getting wrong. But going out with Dutchie had kind of let me in.

"Don't be surprised if nobody talks to you," Diane had warned me on the way to the arena the night I'd met

Dutchie, back in November. I'd looked at her, puzzled. "Nobody knows you yet," she'd explained, making me feel like I'd have to be introduced limb by limb, so as not to scare anyone.

The arena was so cold you could see your breath when you spoke and every word bounced back to hit you in the face. It was where everyone hung out in the winter, sitting on long metal benches that froze your bum, or walking round, stopping to blow fog and print your name on the Plexiglass. It was so different from the back alleys and paths along the water that Jack and I had always played in, pretending we were Samuel de Champlain, the founder of our city. When we were kids, the Saint Lawrence River became the Mississippi and our back lane became Louisiana, which we'd claimed for the king of France.

That night, against all of Diane's predictions, Dutchie came over and talked to me.

"I like your T-shirt," he said, pinching the material around John Lennon's face and pulling me closer.

"Thanks," I said, wondering if this meant we should kiss.

"Where'd you live before?" he asked.

"Verdun."

"Huh?" It was clear he'd never heard of it.

"Did you like it there?"

"It was okay," I said, lying. How would it make me look if I told him I loved it there, that I still woke up every morning missing it?

Dutchie lives in a stone house with a two-car garage that is bigger than our town house and a sunk-in pool in the shape of a large kidney bean. There was nothing like that in Verdun.

I've been going out with Dutchie for six months now and he still doesn't know anything about Jack. We don't really talk much. When I'm at his place, I mostly watch him and his friends gaming or playing pool. I sit on the sofa under the high-powered speakers that are mounted on the wall. Dutchie ripped off the fronts to expose the tweeters and woofers. If I sit under them long enough, my heart syncopates with the beat of the hip-hop bass and I feel as if I too am mounted on the wall, looking down at the pool table. Sometimes, Dutchie will hand me the pool cue and let me take a turn. I always miss and then he slaps my bum, which makes his friends laugh. When they play video games on Dutchie's massive TV that practically takes up the whole back wall, they get so into the action they almost forget I exist, I sit so still and quiet.

～

THE NEXT MORNING the assault was on page two of *The Gazette*. The article didn't mention the fact that Jack was one of the newspaper's delivery boys and that he'd been beaten while working. His route ran along Champlain, parallel to the aqueduct. He was spotted by a man walking his dog at about 7 a.m. Did the editor think the connection was bad for publicity? And if so, was it because of the violence, or because Jack might be gay?

My mother clipped the article and kept rereading it, sniffling into her tissue. I read it only once, holding it at arm's length and scanning the black lines quickly. Because of his age, Jack's name was omitted. They said the victim, who was recovering in the Verdun Hospital, had a severe stutter. I knew Jack's stutter, his machine-gun like repetition of consonants, but I also knew that he only stuttered when people made him nervous, like the kids who made guns of their fingers and imitated him; or my father, who was always angry around Jack.

"You'll have to go over and keep your aunt company this afternoon, Jody," my mom said as she washed the breakfast dishes. So far, she had completely ignored the built-in dishwasher, no matter how many times my father told her to try it.

"Why me?"

"Because one of us should be there. It will make the place seem less empty."

"But why can't you go?"

"Because," my mom replied, leaving it at that. I knew the reason. Neither of us had ever taken the two long bus rides and one short metro ride to Verdun from Dollard. My mom had hardly left the house on her own since we moved. So, it would have to be me.

While I was at my aunt's, two policemen came in to search Jack's room.

"We're trying to find the culprits. Maybe someone threatened him before and he wrote about it or something," one of them said in a heavy French accent. We listened as they opened and shut drawers, pulled books off shelves, books about birds and fish mostly. I knew the insides of Jack's room as well as my own.

Half an hour later they emerged, empty-handed. My aunt, who had spent the whole time twisting a polka-dotted scarf round and round her neck, held back tears as their broad leather shoulders knocked her pictures crooked in the hallway.

"Who would want to hurt Jack?" she asked me.

"I don't know. It was probably strangers, just random violence," I said, taking her hand. I swallowed a lump in my throat. I had hurt Jack too, by abandoning him. Now that I was back there, I knew it. I could feel it in the walls.

When my aunt left for the hospital, I returned home. I didn't want to see Jack in that condition. Besides, he was still out of it and wouldn't have known I was there. That was my excuse for the next month, even when my mother did finally go see Jack, when my father agreed to take her.

Eventually Jack's wounds healed. He never did lose the eye or any fingers to frostbite. But his head hadn't recovered. In January, he was sent to the Douglas Mental Hospital to mend. I couldn't believe he was now inside the big brown hospital that sat beside the river. Jack and I used to cycle past it all the time. We'd stop to watch the attendants, all dressed in white, pushing patients around the wide green lawn in their wheelchairs. How could Jack be one of them?

But he was. And that's where he's been for the last four months, until today.

~

MY AUNT HAS finally come out of her room. Her hair is twisted up in a bun, her body squeezed into a two-piece suit, a flower brooch bursting on the left lapel. The bow of a white blouse is tied tightly under her chin, the loops dangling down her chest. She walks to the center of the room and spins, pivoting on one high-heeled shoe.

"Do I look all right?" she asks and we all nod in unison, even though I think she looks like a high school principal.

I'm wearing jeans and a T-shirt. Every now and then I peek inside my top, amazed at the sight of my cleavage. Sometimes I slip a finger inside and measure its depth. I do this when no one is looking, like while I'm lying on Dutchie's sofa, the sound of pool balls clicking beside me. I wonder what Jack will think when he sees me. I have a sudden flash of the other kids chanting "Jodie and Jackie sitting in a tree, K-I-S-S-I-N-G" when they saw me and Jack together.

Dutchie and I have kissed, but not much more than that. We came close last week. I was helping him count his father's gold. Dutchie's father sells gold charms that come in little plastic bags with ziplock tops. Dutchie wears a replica of everything he owns around his neck: a pool cue, a guitar, a car, a dog. When he started going out with me he added a gold girl.

As I counted, I wondered if the thought of stealing had ever occurred to Dutchie. He and his friends liked to talk tough. They told stories of shoplifting electronic stuff by ripping off the barcodes. And they were always bragging about the million ways they had defied their parents. Their big, daring thrill was to smoke up in the basement then raid Dutchie's fridge upstairs. At times like these, when they were telling their lame stories,

I often felt like spilling the beans about Jack. I bet none of them had a cousin who had actually been beaten up to the point of collapse. Or been the subject of a police investigation, one that still hadn't produced any results.

That day, something about the way Dutchie was counting the bags began to annoy me. I could see him in thirty years, counting bags the same way, his belly a bit fatter but his face still wearing the same smug expression. I don't think Dutchie was even aware of how lucky he was that he'd never have to worry about money. His father was just going to pass the whole business on to him. I thought about Jack and how he worried about where he'd get the money to study to be a vet. He knew it would be tough for his mother, who was a secretary in a small company.

"You could make a lot of money on one of these bags," I blurted out. "Are you ever tempted?"

"You're sick," Dutchie replied, looking at me like I'd just dropped to earth from another planet.

"Sorry," I said, rolling my eyes when he turned away.

Dutchie quit counting bags and sprawled out on the sofa to strum his guitar, jerking his head as though he were on stage. I was suddenly aware of the fact that we were alone for a change. I thought something should happen. Jack and I used to walk along the bushes that border the river late at night, collecting bottles. Once we stumbled on a naked couple, their limbs locked around each other like pretzels. We both turned red and pretended we hadn't seen anything.

I reached out to touch Dutchie's hair, digging my fingers into the long curls. He sat up, kind of startled, staring at me. Then I put my hand around his neck and pulled him towards me. We kissed, slowly at first, and then a bit faster, Dutchie's tongue pushing shyly into my mouth. But when I stretched out to lie down beside him, my foot caught his guitar, knocking it to the floor.

Dutchie jumped up and grabbed it, hugging it to his chest and running his fingers along the strings of the neck. A knob came off in his hands.

"Shit."

"Sorry," I said, straightening up. I just couldn't get anything right in this neighborhood. I had crossed another unseen border.

"Never mind," Dutchie said, replacing the guitar on its stand. "I guess I better give you a lift home."

At my house, I jumped out of the car without saying good-bye and slammed the door. I walked up the driveway, my hand inside my jacket pocket, fingering two gold dice.

~

IT'S FIVE O'CLOCK and Jack is still not here. My stomach is grumbling with anxiety. I've tried to picture this scene a million times, Jack walking in, me running to him. But in my mind we're always alone. I ask Jack to forgive me for not going to visit him. I try to explain why I couldn't. The two neighborhoods were so far apart. Somehow, I couldn't make my way back between them. And besides, from what I'd overheard my mother say on the phone, he wasn't the same Jack anymore. She and my aunt talked about drugs and weight gain and all kinds of things that I couldn't associate with Jack, and that I was afraid to see.

Suddenly, footsteps sound on the inside stairs that lead up to the second-floor. Does Jack still own a key, I wonder, or did they strip away all his personal belongings, like they do to patients in movies? A fist knocks on the door and we all sit still, looking from one to the other. My aunt is back in her bedroom, changing again.

"I'll get it," my father says, rising. My hands are shaking in my lap.

Jack stands in the doorway. He has grown so tall and broad that he almost fills it. He steps inside and scans the room quickly, taking in the balloons and streamers. A slight smile curls the corner of his lips, as if he knew his mother would go overboard.

"Hello, Jack." My father hesitates, then shakes Jack's

hand, the way he would an adult. Jack nods hello. My mother is standing now, reaching up on tippy toes to plant a kiss on Jack's cheek. Then she disappears down the hall. When she comes back my aunt is behind her, stepping shyly, like a child who is being introduced to a room full of adults.

Jack holds out his hand.

"Hello, Mom," he says. My aunt steps forward and they clasp hands and kiss cheeks.

Soon we're all seated with drinks. Jack sits beside my father on the sofa, balanced on the edge, bent forwards with his elbows on his knees. We make small talk about the weather. Nobody mentions the hospital. My aunt, who has changed into a yellow dress, asks whether the living-room looks different? Jack looks around and shakes his head. My aunt jumps up to point out a new shelf with flowery ornaments sitting on it.

"Nice, Mom." Jack smiles.

He hasn't really looked at me yet, only quickly, once or twice. Whenever he does I feel my face flush.

"Well, I think I'll go for a walk and stretch my legs," Jack says suddenly. His stutter has disappeared.

At the door he looks back at me. "Wanna come?"

We turn automatically down the old lane.

"The crazy man still living in the nuthouse?" Jack asks, winking. The crazy man's yard separates Jack's building from my old one. In the summer we used to sneak over the fence and climb the bony-branched crab-apple tree to pluck the rocky green fruit. Once, I slipped a pair under my T-shirt and pretended they were breasts and Jack blushed.

I shrug. The way he says "nuthouse" kind of embarrasses me, considering where he's just come from.

"You're looking good." Jack smiles down on me.

"Thanks," I say, shrugging and blushing. There's so much I want to know, but Jack's good humor throws me off.

"You've changed," I say. Jack grins, as if to say he knows.

"So have you," Jack says.

"I have?" I respond, startled.

"You got a boyfriend?" Jack asks. I meant to keep Dutchie hidden, to keep him on his side of the city, tucked in his square house on the neat street far from the water.

"Yeah," I answer, although Dutchie and I haven't spoken since the night I injured his precious instrument.

Jack nods, as though he had expected this. I want to know where it shows on me. I try to picture myself, holding up a mental mirror. I suppose Dutchie is my proof, but he's not here. The gold dice in my pocket are the only things connecting me to him.

"Hey. Think we could still fit in there?" Jack points to the narrow space between two garages where we used to hide as kids.

"I don't know, but we could try." I once got stuck inside when some kids stuffed cardboard ripped from a refrigerator box in behind me. I couldn't even see the strip of light that was the opening. Jack kept calling "It's okay, I'll get you out" as he pulled out the strips of cardboard like plaster from a cast.

Jack takes my hand and leads me inside the dim space. Our bodies whisk the walls, but we fit.

"Far enough," Jack says. He squeezes his shoulders together and turns to face me. He is outline, shadow; the whites of his eyes are lights. "See, we still fit," he says.

We stare at each other as our eyes grow accustomed to the dark.

"You must be curious," Jack whispers, reading my thoughts. I nod. "There's nothing much to tell," Jack says. Nothing much, only four months in the looney-bin by the river, living under the same roof as the funny-eyed people. And before that, the beating. I see his body lying by the water, curled like a question mark. And the ugly word, *fag*, above him.

"It's over. It's already just a blur, really. I just want to look forward, now that I'm better."

My year is suddenly a blur too. The new neighborhood, the new school, all the new people vanished in this moment with Jack.

"I'm sorry I never came to see you, Jack."

"Oh, forget it. I understand. I wouldn't want to go there either, if I didn't have to. So, how are things?"

Things. That's what Dutchie and Diane seem like now.

"I don't know. I guess I'm doing okay. I'm not too crazy about the new neighborhood. It's different, you know?"

"Yeah, I know." Jack agrees with a sigh that tells me he really does know. I guess his whole life will be different now, after what he's gone through. He'll never again be the person he was before the beating.

"Hey, are you crying?" Jack bends near my face.

Warm tears are trickling into my mouth. There is an ache in my arms and down my chest, as though something that was once there has gone and left nothing but burning skin. The last time I felt understood was here, in this lane, with Jack. Just before moving, I told Jack how much I didn't want to go, and he told me it would all work out and that he'd come visit me often. But then …

Jack bends down and puts his arms tightly around me, pulling me close. This is what I remember about Jack, always feeling good and safe with him, like I was home.

When we separate, Jack says, "Let's get out of here." It's too dark to see his expression.

Back out in the lane, even in the dim May light, I can see how much Jack has changed. The gentle brown eyes are still the same, but his face is sharper. It hits me suddenly that Jack has grown up. If I hadn't moved, and if he hadn't had a breakdown, we probably wouldn't still be playing the same old games anyway.

"You okay?" Jack asks, taking my hand again.

"Yeah," I hesitate. We're almost back at his house and I still feel I don't know anything about him. It's funny how I had pictured Jack coming to rescue me from the new neighborhood. Now I know that won't happen. But I also know that I won't go back to sitting and watching Dutchie, to blending in with the wallpaper, to letting him ignore me except for when he needs me to score points with his friends.

"I guess we should get back now. You know, parents?" Jack says, screwing up his eyebrows.

"You go ahead," I say. "I just have to do something."

"Okay. Are you sure you're all right?" Jack asks.

"I'm okay. Really. I just want to do something first, then I'll be up."

When Jack is gone, I turn and walk towards the aqueduct. It's dark, only the street lights from neighboring roads light the path. But I don't need light. I would know the path blindfolded. I stop on the small footbridge where Jack must have been attacked. I hook my leg over the middle bar. Dutchie's dice are cold tiny ice cubes in my hand. I shake them then release them into the air, high over the silver water.

Then I turn and head back to my cousin Jack's house.

PINK
LADY

Amanda is kneeling on the floor of the hotel room, her elbows on the dusty sill, her nose pressed against the yellowish glass, trying to get a glimpse of New York City at night. She wants to see lights, rows of them strung like sparkling ornaments in the sky, but all she can see is the brick wall of the factory across the street. In the little space of sky that's visible above it, the silver tip of the Chrysler building peeks out. But even that disappears when she stands up, reminding her that she should never have left her father alone yesterday when he checked them in. If she'd been with him, she would have insisted on a room with a view.

"Let's go downstairs for a drink," Amanda says suddenly, holding her bathrobe closed. Her just-washed hair is wrapped in a towel that sits, turban-like, on her head. Her father and her cousin, Franz, refused to use the hotel towels, claiming they smelled musty, but Amanda wants to take in every bit of the New York experience, even the smelly parts. This morning, right in front of them, she drank a glass of cloudy tap water from the bathroom sink, just to prove it.

"Anyone?" she asks again.

Her father and Franz are lying on their twin beds, tired after a long, hot day of walking around Manhattan. Amanda dragged them from one end to the other, from the Village in the south, to the Metropolitan Museum eighty blocks north. They lagged behind, stooped and sweating, while she paraded ahead, calling behind to them every now and then, as if they were lost dogs. All day she had wondered how anyone could not be pumped up in Manhattan. The pulse of the city was like the beat of a drum that kept her moving, but her father and Franz seemed oblivious to its rhythm.

"Come on, Franz. You can watch that dumb show any day. This is *New York*." Franz is watching *Law and Order SVU*, thrilled to see it in its original language and not the dubbed German version he gets back home. She thinks how incredible it is that both she and Franz are eighteen. At times, he seems years younger, and other times way older, as old as her father.

"Come on, Franz." She kicks his feet, which dangle over the edge of his bed, but he still doesn't respond. Amanda finally waves her hand at him, wishing him away. She's beginning to wonder whether she made the right decision to join them on this three-day trip. She'd only said yes because she felt bad for her father. He had just recently moved into his small apartment after he and her mother split up, and two weeks later his German nephew had landed on his doorstep, expecting to be entertained.

"Oh, come on, you guys. What a couple of bores. We can sit home any night and watch TV." Amanda raises her hand into a fist, posing like the Statue of Liberty, a landmark they plan to visit tomorrow.

Suddenly, her father swings his short legs over the side of his bed. "Yeah, okay, you're right. I'll go get washed up," he says, his feet fishing around for his slippers. He slips them on and shuffles into the bathroom.

Amanda is surprised by her father's response. She wasn't expecting him to come, and she isn't sure now that she wants him to. Sitting in a bar with her father might be a little strange. It was really Franz she was trying to motivate. She dresses in the large closet that doubles as her dressing room, putting on the sleeveless, purple dress she bought earlier today at Macy's. A long brass zipper, which she now pulls to just above her breasts, runs up the middle. The material is soft, a kind of fake velvet that turns darker or lighter, depending on how she strokes it. Outside, she tries to capture her reflection in the mirror that hangs on the back of the bathroom door, but the room is so cluttered, with her cot sandwiched between the twin beds, that no matter how she poses, some part of her body is chopped off. When her father comes out of the bathroom, dressed and shaven, her image bangs against the wall, disappearing altogether.

Amanda shifts impatiently from foot to foot as the elevator stops on every floor to collect passengers, the air heavy with perfume and aftershave. She hopes she'll have some kind of adventure, even if it is a small one. After all, how much excitement can she have with her father in tow?

At the lobby everyone files out. Amanda envies the people spinning out through the revolving doors into the glittering Manhattan night. With a sigh, she turns toward the hotel lounge, her father following close behind. The bar is pitch-black, except for a circle of light that catches the crystal glasses that hang upside down around the bar. A dozen round tables are scattered around the room and, from somewhere off in a dimly lit corner, the sound of a woman's voice singing a bluesy song fills the air.

Amanda watches her father flop into a chair before

sitting down herself. Over the years, his once athletic body has grown pudgy. His face, since the breakup, wears a dull gaze that doesn't penetrate anything further than two feet away. He sits nervously, elbows on the table, thumbs circling each other. When he nibbles his nails, Amanda looks away. She imagines her father's future as a long and lonely one. She sees him grow fatter and duller year by year, eating nothing but take-out in front of the TV in his undershirt.

Their waiter approaches, wearing a black waistcoat, white shirt, and red bowtie. Amanda smiles, letting her glance linger on his face as he sets napkins before them. She's praying he won't ask for I.D. Eighteen may be legal drinking age at home, in Montreal, but she's not sure if it is New York.

"What will you have?" he asks, fixing his glance somewhere between them.

"I'll have a Pink Lady, please," Amanda responds quickly, wanting to be first. She's never had one of these before, but she remembers someone ordering one in a movie. It was served in a tall, elegant glass and that's how she feels tonight, tall and elegant, even if she is only with her father.

"And you, sir?"

Amanda's father stops biting his nails and mumbles, "Umm, give me a ..."

Amanda straightens in her chair. Her father's shyness makes her want to squeeze his neck to pop the words out. "Bring him a Singapore Sling," she answers for him. She gives the waiter a sharp look and he smiles back, obviously amused.

Two men are sitting at the bar, hunched over their drinks. Occasionally, one rotates his head from side to side to scan the mirror, as if he's expecting someone to materialize behind him.

The waiter returns with the drinks. "Do you want to pay now or should I let it run?" he asks.

"Oh, let it run," Amanda blurts out. She looks back at the bar and thinks she recognizes one of the men as the chauffeur on their bus tour yesterday. She leans back and stretches her neck but can't see his face properly. In the mirror that runs behind the bar, his face is doubled and distorted in a bottle of Canadian Club.

Amanda starts to point him out to her father, but he's completely absorbed in the music, swaying his head from side to side. Amanda scans the room, looking for the source of the music, and finds a woman sitting at a white grand piano. She has long black hair that falls over bare shoulders, and her dress must have sequins or rhinestones sewn into it because she sparkles when she moves.

Amanda suddenly wonders if her father has spent much time in hotel bars. After all, he does travel a lot for work.

In fact, he was away more than home the whole time she was growing up. She has always pictured him sitting alone in cramped motel rooms, ones where the sheets are worn thin and the TV sets play nothing but static.

"Do you like the drink?" She shakes his glass in front of his face to catch his attention.

"Hmm? Yeah, it's good." He takes a long sip, his mouth gripping the side of the glass where the yellow umbrella floats. Amanda chuckles at the way he doesn't know that he's supposed to take it out first. A minute later, he bangs his glass on the table and, to Amanda's surprise, says, "So, what should I have next?"

Amanda leans forward, drawing her legs and arms together. "Next? Well, let's see. How about a Bloody Caesar?" She raises her long, slender arm, liking the way her silver bangles tingle as they slide toward her elbow. As the waiter approaches, she decides he's definitely handsome, in spite of the wrinkles and gray sideburns. She imagines he lives in an apartment bordering the East River, the kind with an outside terrace, like the ones they drove by yesterday on the tour.

"Could we have a Bloody Caesar, please?"

Amanda's father is smiling to himself, staring at his clasped hands. Then he turns his head toward the piano player, slouching down even further in his chair. The music stops and the woman stands up. Now Amanda can see that a thick silver belt gathers her long, black dress around a very slim waist. At the sound of applause, the piano lady bows slightly. Amanda's father pulls himself straight and claps loudly, continuing long after everyone else has stopped and the piano lady has stepped off into the shadows.

"Dad, you don't have to go haywire," Amanda says, glaring at him.

"Why not? She was great," her father replies. Amanda can't remember her father ever showing any musical appreciation before.

The waiter brings the new drink, which is the color of blood. The man whom Amanda thinks was the tour bus driver moves a few stools closer. She sees him clearly now in the mirror over the sink. His eyes are deep brown and his lips are full, and wet with drink. She catches his eyes but can't tell if he's looking at her because the mirror is bumpy and it looks as though each eye is staring off into a different direction. Amanda recalls the streets they'd driven through near the docks yesterday to get back to the hotel, blocks of dilapidated buildings and empty lots where girls in mini-skirts leaned against poles and fences. Some of them were so young they were still flat-chested, and they walked slowly on their five-inch heels, as if angered at having to move.

Amanda's father couldn't believe the driver had chosen that route. "Surely there are better sights to see," he said. But Amanda defended the driver. "It's all part of the city, Dad. You can't just pretend the ugly parts don't exist." Franz, for his part, was too busy retracing their route on his map to take in any of the details.

Amanda's father is ready for round three.

"What should I have next?" he asks.

She doesn't know what to say. Why is he asking her? Why doesn't he order himself? When the waiter reaches their table, Amanda has a sudden inspiration. She straightens up and asks, "Do you have any Zombies here?"

"Certainly, Miss," the waiter responds, grinning. Even her father chuckles. She had meant to sting him, but he's smiling instead.

When the drink comes, Amanda stares at the slices of orange and lemon that hug the lip of her father's glass. Then she watches him down the entire Zombie in a couple of easy gulps. Her Pink Lady is still half full. There's no way she can keep up.

The piano player returns and plays with even more intensity, swooping so low over the keys she's almost kissing them. Amanda turns to make sure the bus driver is still there and he tips his glass to her in the mirror. Amanda wishes she could find a delicate way of asking her father to leave, but when she looks at him she sees that he's completely enraptured by the music. His eyes are glued to the piano player, the way Franz's are probably glued to the television set seven floors up. Finally, the music stops, but this time Amanda's father doesn't clap. He gets up instead, much to Amanda's relief.

"I'm going to go now," he says without looking at her. He tries to push his chair in behind him but it keeps banging into the table legs. Amanda stifles a giggle, thinking of the odd mixture of drinks he has consumed. She pictures him and Franz upstairs, passed out on their narrow beds. Finally, he abandons the chair and throws Amanda two twenty-dollar bills. "This should be enough. I'll see you later," he says, walking away into the dark.

The table is suddenly too big for one person. Amanda takes a long sip, finishing off her Pink Lady. Then she moves over to the bar, centering herself on a stool so that her cheeks are not deformed and bloated in the bumpy mirror.

"Hi," the bus driver says, nodding.

"Hi," she says back. "I think I was on your tour bus yesterday."

He keeps staring, his face blank. "Oh, yeah, sure," he says finally, sucking an ice cube. "You staying in this hotel?"

"Yeah."

"What were you drinking?"

"A Pink Lady."

"A Pink Lady? Very fancy, huh?" He laughs and Amanda smiles nervously. "Another scotch and a Pink Lady, Sam." When she turns to look at him, a loud hiccup escapes her lips.

"Too much to drink, huh?" he says. She half smiles and hiccups again. "Here, have another one." As he passes her the drink, his hand brushes the skin above her breasts, where the zipper ends.

The waiter who served them all evening carries a tray of dirty glasses behind the bar. He nods to the bus driver and Amanda is sure he's smirking as he bends under the counter.

"You here alone?" the bus driver asks her.

"Yes." The second Pink Lady seems more potent than the first. Amanda pivots her stool to face the driver.

"A young girl all alone in New York City," he says, his breath heavy with the antiseptic smell of scotch. Earlier in the day, such a title would have thrilled her. Now, she isn't sure.

"Who was that guy you were with before?" he asks. This time when he speaks she notices the black holes in his front teeth.

"Oh, nobody," she says, dismissing her father with a casual wave of her hand. The waiter walks by wearing jeans and a brown checked shirt. He waves at the bus driver who nods back and says, "Night, Sam."

"Where's he going?" Amanda asks. It seems incredible that he would just change in the middle of an evening and walk out.

"Home, I guess?"

Amanda thinks of the elegant terraced apartments by the East River. "Where's his home?" she asks.

"I don't know. Somewhere in the Bronx, I think. Why?"

"The Bronx!" Amanda has never been to the Bronx but she can't associate it with anything glamorous or exciting.

"Who cares where he lives anyway, babe. How about you coming home with me? That's more interesting, don't you think?"

Amanda watches him grin. It's the same grin he wore as they drove through the run-down blocks, the same grin that swept over the young hookers. For some reason, Amanda pictures the waiter sitting on the dirty subway on his way home to a cramped apartment in the Bronx, and her spirits dampen. She has heard the bus driver's question and doesn't know what to say. Of course she can't go off with him. What does he think? But she doesn't want her hesitation to show. She doesn't want him to know that she has never handled an offer like this before. But, what if he becomes insistent? What if she can't get away from him? Suddenly she remembers that her father has returned to their hotel room. Surely he'll look at his watch and realize how late it is. He'll force Franz to tear his eyes away from the television set and come get her. He wouldn't just forget about her down here. He always keeps in touch when he's on the road, even now, even if it's just a quick text to say good morning or goodnight. Amanda thinks of pulling out her phone to see if there's a message but how could she explain it if the bus driver asked her what she was looking for?

The man snaps his fingers near Amanda's nose, pulling her back to the present. She feels him poised on the edge of his stool, awaiting a reply, but when she looks at the mirror she realizes that he's facing the front entrance. Slowly, his face breaks into a smile. The blacks of his teeth really show now, like two dark pits. He's staring across the room at the open door. Two figures, lit by the light of the lobby, are caught in the frame.

"Hey, isn't that the guy you were with before?" he asks, nodding in their direction.

Amanda's Pink Lady slips from her hand, the long stem sliding between her fingers. Cold liquid pours between her breasts as she looks over to see her father, his pudgy arm secure around the slender waist of the piano lady.

SMART
ALECK

The back door clicks open and the sound of peanuts hitting the patio reaches Ruth where she's lying in her bedroom. She kicks off her blanket, swings her legs over the bed, and leans over her bureau to look out the window. Four fat squirrels are gathered around a cluster of peanuts. Ruth listens to her mother call to the squirrels, making a clucking noise with her tongue that sounds like *te-te-te*. Ruth shudders, thinking how her mother always manages to make herself appear naive. In her mind, she sees the way her mother would now be shaking her head from side to side, her long reddish hair flopping in her face.

Ruth has tried to make her mother hate the squirrels by telling her they're rats, nothing but rats with tails.

They have the same instincts, and as far as she's concerned, they all belong in sewers. But Ruth's mother still treats her as though she should care about the creatures. She'll even call Ruth over to the window to watch the squirrels eat.

"Hurry, they're leaving," she'll say. Ruth walks slowly, to emphasize that she couldn't care less. When the squirrels' soft brown eyes look up at her she always says, "Rats" and walks away.

Ruth watches as more squirrels scurry down the trees to gather nuts. A white plastic bird bath sits on the patio and several sparrows are perched on the edge, dipping their beaks into the water. Ruth's mother sent her to the hardware store at the shopping mall to buy the bird bath last week. Ruth cursed the whole way there and took the quiet streets home so that no one would see her carrying the bird bath, which was too big to fit in any shopping bag.

Ruth throws her arms into the sleeves of her yellow bathrobe and ties it around her large frame as she stamps down the hallway to the kitchen.

"What are you doing?" she snaps at her mother.

"Nothing, honey. Just watching the squirrels. Some of them are turning white already," her mother responds, as though Ruth cares about their color.

Ruth sticks out her chin, furrows her brows, and

slams down the button on the toaster. She bangs the kettle onto a gas burner and, as the fire spreads out under it, says, "Who cares? They're rats."

"Oh, Ruth," her mother replies gently. None of Ruth's outbursts seem to bother her mother, and this makes Ruth want to lash out even more. She sometimes feels that her mother is a balloon that she is blowing air into, daring it to burst.

The whistle blows on the kettle, sending steam into the air. Ruth pours boiling water into a coffee filter that sits on her special mug. On it is a picture of a yellow bird holding a diploma above the words, *Smart Aleck*. She won the mug at school, for writing the best essay in her Social Studies class. Her topic was "Assertiveness and the Passive Woman," a topic Ruth feels like an expert on. Ruth often thinks about how this mug proves that she and her mother are different. She's assertive in a way her mother never could be. Whenever she looks at the mug, she feels relieved. She won't live her life slaving away for others as her mother has. As Ruth stares at her mother's back, she sees herself running away, leaving her mother way behind in her chair where she sits, day after day, looking out into the yard, like the goddess of a kingdom, watching over her creatures. It's the only job she has.

Ruth's toast pops up, snapping her out of her

daydream. Her mother draws her face away from the window and says, "There's some good marmalade in the pantry, Ruth. I got it yesterday at Laura Secord's."

Ruth drops the slightly burned toast on a plate. "I don't like marmalade. I never have," she says, as she carries her plate and mug over to the table. You'd think that after seventeen years her own mother would know her taste.

"Oh, sorry," her mother says, turning to stare out at the yard again.

"Yuck. This coffee tastes like crap," Ruth declares, after taking her first sip.

"Oh Ruth, it's not that bad."

"It is too. No wonder the girl wanted to get rid of it." Ruth remembers the girl who came to the door to sell it yesterday. She wore a pressed white shirt, navy vest and skirt, and carried a shiny black briefcase. Ruth boils when she thinks of the astonished smile that spread over the girl's face when her mother agreed to buy a jar of the coffee, which had supposedly been made by a non-profit organization in Brazil. She pictures the peasants slaving away to pick the beans and some fat plantation owner chuckling all the way to the bank.

Ruth drinks the coffee anyway, because it's there and she needs the boost. Her toast would taste better with marmalade, but there's no way of getting it now. She watches her mother's eyes circling the back yard and thinks how unbelievable it is that anyone could spend so much time worrying about silly creatures.

"Those squirrels and birds make such a mess out there with all their cracked shells. I hate it," Ruth says, taking her dishes to the sink.

Her mother just shrugs, so Ruth strides down the hall to her room, sits at her desk, and stares at her reflection in the black screen of her laptop. She combs back her yellow hair and thinks how lucky she is to be so pretty, with her green eyes, small nose, and full-lipped mouth, which always curves upwards in a confident smile. She doesn't even need make-up. It's the face of a person destined to be independent and to have an important job, one with many people working under her. The only job Ruth remembers her mom doing the whole time she was growing up was at a co-op daycare where she looked after other people's kids two days a week. Even that job had ended after a few years. People often tell Ruth she looks like her mother, but it isn't true. Her mother's eyes are blue and her hair is red, not yellow.

The doorbell rings and Ruth hears her mother's slippers shuffling along the hall. She peeks around the door frame and sees Rachel, her hair swept up in a high bun that looks like a beehive, standing on the other side of the fishnet curtains. Fat little Jamie clings to her legs, his mouth open as though he's whining. "Brat," murmurs Ruth.

"I hope you're not busy," Rachel says.

"Oh, no, not at all," Ruth's mother responds. "Can I get you a coffee?"

"Okay. I've got some time to waste," Rachel replies. "It's getting so damn cold I won't be able to leave the house soon. Then what'll I do? I'll be stuck in the house with him."

Ruth pictures Jamie crawling along the black and white tiles to the kitchen cupboards. Every time he comes over he pulls out all the Tupperware that the Greek lady down the street managed to sell to Ruth's mother. The more destructive he got, the shinier his eyes grew, as though he had never enjoyed such freedom.

"I'm sorry I've no nice treats to offer you. I really need to do a shopping."

Ruth winces. She can't stand hearing her mother apologize to Rachel. Rachel should consider herself lucky that she's been allowed past the front door so early in the morning. Ruth would never have let her in that far. She wonders if the reference to shopping was her mother's subtle way of telling Rachel she did have things to do.

"That's okay," says Rachel. "Jamie can eat later and the last thing I need is any more calories." Rachel chuckles at her own wit and Ruth pictures her patting her stomach.

Ruth's mother met Rachel last summer when she came over to complain about the caterpillars that were crawling off their tree and into Rachel's house through the back porch. She suggested that Ruth's mother call an exterminator, but Ruth knew that her mother couldn't stand to see any creature hurt, not even ones that crawled. Finally, Ruth's father, who agreed with Rachel that the caterpillars had gotten out of hand, took care of them himself, burning the cottony nests with fire-rags tied to the end of a mop handle. Every time a group of ashes fell to the ground, Rachel raised her fist in victory. Ruth's mother stayed inside, far from her usual post at the window, during the operation. Afterwards, Rachel came over with Jamie to thank her, but now she couldn't stop coming.

"Jamie, stop it!" Rachel commands, without any authority in her voice. "He's such a bugger," she adds, chuckling. Ruth cringes at the crashing and scraping sounds that echo down the hall. Jamie must be making another Tupperware tower.

"Oh, don't worry about it, Rachel. The floor's dirty anyway," Ruth's mother says, which isn't true. Their floor is never dirty because Ruth's mother washes and polishes it once a week.

"I get so fed up of staying in the house all day. And this guy —" Jamie gurgles loudly, like he's driving something along the floor. "I wish I could send him to daycare, but they won't take him until he's two. Five months to go." Jamie bangs more plastic, as if he's responding to his mother's eagerness to be rid of him.

Ruth starts slowly down the hall, waiting to hear what will come next. She has to go to school, but she can't leave her mother alone with Rachel. When she steps into the kitchen she sees Rachel playing with a hair curl which loops around her ear like a snail. Her mother is making her way through the Tupperware to pour their coffee at the counter.

"Here you go," Ruth's mother's voice squeaks. The coffee runs down her hands, hot with steam. "Oops, I'm sorry. It spilled."

Ruth grinds her teeth.

"Oh, it's okay. There's enough left," Rachel says.

Ruth stamps along the kitchen floor, kicking Tupperware out of her way to make a path to the sink.

"I don't know if you'll like it," Ruth's mother says.

"Why? What kind is it?"

Ruth turns the tap on full-force and tries not to listen. She glares down at Jamie, who sits cross-legged in the midst of his Tupperware Empire, grinning like a CEO counting his cash. "Brat," she reminds herself.

"I don't really know. I bought it yesterday. This young lady was selling it to raise money."

"Oh!" Rachel sets her cup down, hard. Ruth watches the beehive on Rachel's head shake as though real bees are whirring around inside, waiting to be released. "She came to my door too, but I never buy from people like that. You don't know if you can trust them. I just slam the door on them."

"Well, it seemed like a good cause," Ruth's mother responds apologetically.

Ruth glares at Rachel. Jamie tears a magnetic lady bug off the fridge and throws it into a plastic bowl. Ruth bends down, retrieves it, and slams it back onto the fridge, higher up. How will they deal with Jamie in three or four years, when he's taller? Ruth shivers. But she won't be here then, she reminds herself. She suddenly wants to take an ax and slice off Rachel's beehive.

Rachel raises the cup of coffee cautiously to her lips. Ruth's mother's small frame is curved delicately in her chair, but her eyes are distant, as though she has removed herself from the scene. A cold chill runs through Ruth's entire body as she watches Rachel scrunch up her face in disgust, as if to say the coffee tastes like crap. Two pictures flash in Ruth's mind: one of herself and the other of Rachel, her brown curls plastered against her head like swirls in a stucco pattern.

She and Rachel have the same expression in their eyes. Again, Ruth wants to take an ax and chop off the ridiculous bun that's fifty years out of fashion. She wants to watch it fall to the ground in a million pieces, like the ashes of the caterpillar nests.

"She thought *she* had it hard," Rachel says, her high-pitched voice calling Ruth back to reality.

Jamie shoots a cup at Ruth's leg to get her out of his way. Ruth cups her hands around her mouth so that no one will see and sticks her tongue out at him. Then she pulls a chair close to her mother and sits down. She'll just stay for a few minutes then head up to school, where she's preparing a debate with her team on the topic of "Ten Commandments for the Postmodern World." Ruth thinks how the first one should be: *Don't let annoying neighbors into your life.*

"She had all those millions, and maids, and chauffeurs, and still she was unhappy. I'd trade places with her in minute," Rachel's voice continues to buzz. Ruth has no idea who she's talking about, but she knows it isn't someone her mother would care about. The lives of the rich and famous don't interest her at all; she only cares about her backyard creatures.

Suddenly, Ruth's mother cranes her neck forward and turns her head slowly, as though she's following something. Ruth looks out the window and sees a black cat creeping along the top of the picket fence that separates this house from Rachel's, slinking along as though it's sneaking up on some prey.

"She thought she had it hard, she should try being cooped up with him all day. She should come to live at my house." Rachel clutches at a gold chain around her neck as she talks, as though it is somehow holding her back. "She's just a trashy go-getter." As Rachel says this, Ruth's mother leans forward, a rare mean slant closing over her left eye. "Chauffeurs, expense accounts, trips around the world." Rachel's high bun draws a circle in the air.

Ruth's mother nods, but she's barely listening. All her attention centers on the black cat, which has stopped beside the tree, above the bird bath.

"Meeting all those famous people." Jamie is throwing the cups and bowls against the counter, punctuating his mother's words, as though they're complaining together. "I wouldn't give a damn either what all the newspapers had to say. I would've left him, too, and gone for the money. You gotta do what you gotta do in this world."

The black cat crouches onto its hind legs, its eyes concentrating on whatever it's looking at.

"I saw her picture online, dancing at some fancy club in New York, eating caviar and drinking champagne.

That's the way to do it, fling yourself at every opportunity."

The black cat leaps off the fence and, almost simultaneously, Ruth's mother springs out of her chair. She runs out the back door and starts screaming, "Shoo, get out of here, shoo," as she claps her hands. Rachel and Jamie run to the window together, their eyes wide with astonishment, like they're watching a freak show. Jamie wraps his fat arms around his mother's legs, as though he's afraid she's going to run outside and start screaming too. Rachel is laughing and shaking her head in disbelief. Ruth has never hated Rachel more than at that minute. She wants to yell at her, to tell her to stop gawking at her mother that way, as if she has a right to judge. If only she could have cut off Rachel's beehive. Then Ruth would have known that no one can stand in her way, that no one can stop her from leaving her mother and her animals behind. But that hasn't happened.

Rachel's nose is now scrunched up, as though she smells something rotten. A mocking grin stretches above her chin. The bees buzz in her bun, and Ruth hears the buzz travel over the air as Rachel tells the neighbors that the lady who feeds the birds and squirrels is crazy. *I was there, I saw it with my own eyes*, she'll buzz.

Finally, Ruth's mother is quiet. Ruth fixes her eyes on the back door as her mother steps into the kitchen.

Her face is white and her eyes, still distant, don't move. Ruth feels herself panic when she looks down at her mother's hands. Cupped gently in her palms, lies a baby squirrel. The skin on its back is torn and blood runs down its body, over her mother's hands, and drips onto the floor. The squirrel's mouth hangs open. Two pointy teeth stare up at Ruth — harmless, as tiny as grains of rice.

"Ooo, gross," Rachel exclaims, as she crams herself into the corner, clutching her gold chain again. "How can you touch that?"

Ruth's mother doesn't answer. She lays the squirrel down on a dish towel and wraps its body. Then she looks up at Rachel with cold, blue eyes that sparkle with rage. As her mother glares at Rachel, Ruth finally sees the beehive fall to the ground. Rachel grabs her sweater off the back of her chair, yanks Jamie's hand and runs with him down the hall and out the front door. Ruth's mother's eyes follow her the whole way.

Ruth pushes her chair back, gets up and, with her arms wrapped tightly around herself, approaches her mother. She reaches one shaky hand toward her, wanting to touch her somehow. She brushes the edge of her mother's shoulder and opens her mouth hesitantly, as if she's speaking to her for the very first time. But when her mother turns to face her, the cold blue in her eyes hasn't melted.

LORI WEBER

Ruth watches her mother open her mouth and shrinks back.

"Rat," her mother says, her voice steady, barely above a whisper. Then she carries the blood-soaked dish towel out the back door. Ruth hears her mother mumble, "How can anyone say they're rats?"

Ruth sinks to the floor, landing in the midst of Jamie's abandoned empire. Her nose is running, but she doesn't wipe it. Her eyes are glued to the counter. Her special mug sits there, looking down at her. The words *Smart Aleck* hit her like a dagger at the exact same second that her mother lowers the dead squirrel into the ground.

RELATIVITY

"We tend to think of time as being fixed and linear, but, in fact, time and space are relative to each other," says my father. "For example, if you were traveling in a train that was moving at the speed of light, you would no longer be part of the time going on outside the train, so that when you arrived at the station, you would be younger than anyone who was traveling outside the train in normal time."

As he talks, my mind drifts. I picture myself sitting in some supersonic turbo train, whipping past green, blurry fields. We travel so fast the cows are smears of black and white and when we get to the station I'm a baby again. If the train travels fast enough, I'm not even born. My mother is twenty-five, just married to my father, who was forty-five at the time. Or even younger and still working at the hair salon where my father came in for a cut and later courted her with newly refurbished curling irons and blow-dryers.

"Now you explain it to me," he says when he's finished.

"I can't, Dad," I reply. It isn't fair that he expects me to. None of my friends know the theory of relativity.

"You have to pay attention, Alberta. You'll never learn anything if you don't. You have to work hard and with maximum effort. Then you'll be remembered for great things, like Einstein."

Einstein is my father's hero. He's always pointing out his genius and reminding me that Einstein worked in the same field as him: electricity. Well, at least that's the field Einstein started off in. Plus, they were both born in Europe and moved to North America when they were older. He makes it sound like they're brothers or something. My dad even has white bushy hair that springs out from behind his ears and two white tufts of hair that twist out of his nostrils, like Einstein. People stare when I'm with him, which I don't like.

He's been trying to teach me the theory of relativity forever and, now that I'm fifteen, I'm sick of it.

"Come on, Alberta," he says again. "Try."

"No, Dad. I don't care," I spit back. My father just

looks at me, stunned, then he shuffles off to his work-room, as though he can't stand to be near me. As I watch him walk away, I think about my best friend, Camille, who escaped for the summer. She found a job as an au pair for a family that owns a lakeside cottage in the Laurentian Mountains. While I'm being grilled about Einstein, she's probably sun-tanning on the shore of some picturesque lake. Camille has all the luck. She has young parents who throw wild parties where people dance until morning. Her mother laughs the whole time, shaking her breasts exaggeratedly inside skimpy tops, a move that would mortify my mother. My mom is so proper that when she hangs out laundry in the summer, she hides our bras under towels.

∽

I'M SITTING OUTSIDE the next day when a moving van pulls up across the street. The back door swings open and a couple of men begin hauling out furniture. It's cheap stuff, busted-up, like you find in the back of Value Village, buried under inches of dust. None of the kitchen chairs match and the bed-frames look ancient. Even though my mother isn't with me, I can hear her tutting and sighing.

A minute later a red car pulls up behind the truck, also screeching to a halt. A woman wearing a bright orange T-shirt springs out of the driver's seat and hops onto the sidewalk. She stands there, looking around, then lets out a huge laugh, as though she's just seen something hilarious.

"This is it, kids. Come on. You can't stay in the car for the rest of your lives," she calls out. Then she laughs again. The sound echoes between the high brick triplexes that run up and down our street. I've never heard a grown-up laugh like that. When my mother laughs, she always covers her mouth, as if she's doing something wrong.

The rest of the car doors open, and three young kids jump out.

"Don't forget the baby," the woman calls.

The biggest boy, who looks about five, scoops a baby out of the back seat and holds it up to his mother, like a package.

"You take her, Ma," he says.

"No, Sweetie. She's all yours. I have to supervise." Then she disappears inside the bottom flat.

The boy saunters up to the low wooden fence that surrounds the tiny yard and plunks the baby down in the high grass. Then he runs away, followed by two younger sisters. The grass swallows the baby right up, like a beast. No one has done any maintenance over there since the last tenants left in February, when the yard was still buried under hard-packed snow.

A minute later the mother reappears. "Have they left you all alone, little Annie?" she says, looking down at the baby, who's trying to part the grass with her head. "Don't worry. Mama's here." Then she turns around and disappears again.

The moving men are now carrying a brown sofa on their shoulders, like a coffin. One of its legs falls off and rolls into the gutter, landing a foot away from a sewer opening. I cross the street, pick up the wooden leg and head toward the house. The second I step near the yard, the baby starts to gag, her entire mouth stuffed with grass. It hangs out of her lips like long green whiskers.

I don't know what to do, so I climb over the fence and pick her up, still clutching the sofa leg.

"Let's get that yucky grass out of your mouth," I say. Then I scoop, hoping my fingers don't have germs. They shouldn't have. The most high-powered microscope, even one invented by Einstein himself, couldn't find a germ in my house, and that's in spite of the fact that my mother cuts old ladies' hair in our spare room. I wipe another wet glob of grass onto my jean shorts. "There. Done."

Just then the mother steps outside. "Well, Annie-belly. I see you've made a friend already. Hi, I'm Angela. Angela Dwight. Who are you?"

"Alberta," I say, hating my name. It tells everyone the obvious — my father wanted a boy and the best he could do was stick an "a" at the end of Albert. I wonder if he even knows that Einstein and his wife abandoned their baby daughter.

"Alberta? Well now. Do you live next door to Saskatchewan?" Mrs. Dwight says. Then she throws her head way back and cracks up. There are wide spaces between her front teeth, as though years of laughing have caused them to separate.

"Sorry, honey. I didn't mean to tease. Have you seen my other kids?"

"They kind of ran off," I say.

"Little rats. They'll come back when they're hungry. They always do."

I wait for her to ask for Annie, but she doesn't.

"Well, you two have fun. I've got lots to do."

My mouth falls open as I watch her go back inside. Annie is looking at me, her eyes wide open. If she could speak, she'd be begging me not to abandon her to the wild grass again. The neighborhood dogs even use this yard as a toilet. So, I keep hold of her and settle on the front stoop, away from the entrance, so that the moving men can still come and go. I jiggle her around a bit and, as I do, I realize this is the first time I've ever held a baby. I've touched a few before, stroking a fat cheek, but this is the first one to nestle in my arms.

To my surprise, Annie falls fast asleep, snug against

my chest. I watch the movers, who are on to boxes now, ones with dishes and clothes bursting out the tops. About half an hour later they finish and the moving van leaves. The other children wander back, and Annie wakes up and starts to howl.

I have to find this baby's mother, so I decide to go inside, uninvited. My mother would definitely not approve.

"Oh, there you are Alberta," Mrs. Dwight says. "I was wondering when you were going to bring Annie in. The changing stuff is there, on the table. I just unpacked it."

I follow Mrs. Dwight's finger to the kitchen table, which is stacked with diapers and other baby paraphernalia, like wipes and powder. Does she really expect me to change a diaper? I don't know how, and Annie is not my baby.

"But ..." I start to say.

"I know, I know. She might not need a new one. But let's give her one anyway. Okay?" Then she vanishes down the hallway. I hear her call out, "When you're done, we can try to organize lunch."

Now I'm starting to panic. Who does she think I am — Mary Poppins?

Annie's big brown eyes stare up at me and a smile spreads across her face, two tiny white teeth sticking up from her lower gums.

"Okay, okay. But just this time," I say softly. I lay Annie down on the table and undress her, trying not to stare at her naked body. Even though she's just a baby, it doesn't seem right. It isn't that hard to change a diaper, once I figure out all the snaps and tabs and things. Thankfully, it's only pee.

There's no crib or playpen in sight, so I carry Annie outside with me. The other kids are gone again.

"Here," I say, offering Annie to Mrs. Dwight. "She's changed. I've got to go."

"Oh, I see," she says, scratching her rust-colored hair. It's pulled into a lopsided ponytail, with loose pieces springing out all over the place. I notice, for the first, time, what huge boobs she has. They're practically spilling out of her orange T-shirt. I also notice that the orange is mostly juice stains.

"Well, what time can you start tomorrow?" she asks, plunking Annie back in the yard.

"Start?" I ask, wondering if I should warn her about the dog poop.

"Yeah, you know. When can you get here? This lot gets going awfully early."

"But I ..."

"I mean, you want the job, don't you?" Mrs. Dwight asks. "I'll pay you and you look like you know what you're doing. These kids won't give you any trouble."

"But I'm not looking —"

"Oh, thank God," Mrs. Dwight says suddenly, look-ing over my shoulder. I turn to see a taxi pulling up to the curb. A man gets out and Mrs. Dwight claps her hands. "Thank God," she exclaims again, bouncing in her flip-flops.

I want to explain that she made a mistake. I didn't come for work. I just happened to notice the leg fall off the sofa and then Annie eating grass. But when the man turns around, all my thoughts vanish. The words turn to mush in my mouth.

Standing in front of me is the most gorgeous guy I've ever seen. He's tall and muscular and tanned, with black wavy hair that falls into sky blue eyes, high cheek-bones, and a wide mouth surrounded by a mustache and small beard.

All three kids jump on him and he catches them, no problem. If my father tried that, he'd break his back.

"I'll be over at seven," I say, without taking my eyes off Mr. Dwight.

But Mrs. Dwight doesn't hear me. She's too busy laughing. Mr. Dwight looks my way and my breath catches. I want to attract Mrs. Dwight's attention and tell her I've changed my mind. I can help out with lunch after all, and supper too. I don't really need to go home. What will I do there? Watch my mom vacuum up the snippets of gray hair that get trailed from the spare room down the hall to the front door when the old ladies leave. Sometimes, I think she and that machine have fused, like the hose is an extension of her arm. But the entire family is now heading toward their new house, the kids forming a chain anchored to Mr. Dwight's leg. His arm is around Mrs. Dwight's shoulder while she leans her head against his chest.

Doesn't he see the stains on her shirt?

As they pass the yard, Mr. Dwight scoops up Annie with one big hand. She squeals with glee as she travels through the air to her father's shoulder.

I stand there watching, transfixed. I want to be Mrs. Dwight and Annie all at once. I want to fly through the air, laughing out loud as I land on Mr. Dwight's broad shoulder. And I want to be held like Mrs. Dwight, with my head resting on Mr. Dwight's chest.

"Alberta!" My mother's voice slices through the air like an arrow. I look across the street to see her shaking a towel over the banister. When she's done, the white hairs lay curled in the grass like slugs. My mother is constantly shedding hair and dust and dirt, removing germs. If she's having something delivered, like the day the new washing machine came, she lays newspaper along the hallway. I could hear the men cursing under their breath as they slid and tripped on the sheets.

I want to follow the Dwights into their new house. I want to become part of their family and hide away from my mother and her chores, and my father and his lectures on Einstein.

But the Dwights' door slams shut and I have nowhere to go but home.

⸙

I GO OVER to the Dwights' every morning at seven and stay until four. I play with the kids, wash their faces, feed them lunch, stick bandages over their scrapes, and do all the other things any normal mother would do. Mrs. Dwight does nothing. At about eight o'clock every morning, she pulls a ripped plastic chair down the hall from the kitchen and plunks herself in it, tipping her chin to the sun. If Annie cries, she opens one eye and tells me to check on her, like I wouldn't have thought of that myself.

Nobody mentions anything about money after that first day, but I don't care. The payoff for my work is the daily return of Mr. Dwight. I watch him sauntering down the street from the bus stop, his heavy-duty lunch pail swinging by his thighs, which are packed into tight and perfectly faded jeans. The kids run to meet him, their arms wrapping around his strong legs, and he lifts them one by one and helicopter-rides them down the street.

I always turn away when he runs up the steps and kisses Mrs. Dwight. I can't understand how they can be related, if married couples can be considered related. I look from one to the other, trying to fit them together, but I can't. In my mind, they repel each other, like magnets turned backward.

I also wonder whether Mr. Dwight is aware of the chaos in which his wife is raising his children. I suppose he can't really know, since he's away all day, working machines that roll up miles of wire fence. Bits and pieces of those rolls dot the Dwights' backyard, rising out of the gravel like strange modern sculptures. He even used some of the fencing to line Annie's play-yard, which he also cleaned up.

Occasionally, I linger for a few minutes, but Mr. Dwight barely notices me. He darts a quick glance in my direction, then goes into the house. That's Mrs. Dwight's signal to pull her plastic chair inside and gather her children. Then the entire Dwight clan disappears until after supper.

↬

I BEGIN TO notice that every morning, at about ten o'clock, Mrs. Dwight rises from her plastic throne and enters the flat. One day, Darren just happens to be close by.

"Darren, where's your mom going?" I ask.

"Mommy's feeding Daddy's fish," he replies.

"What fish?" I ask, convinced he's lying. But he's already off on his bike, out of reach. I have never seen any fish in the Dwights' flat.

The next day I follow Mrs. Dwight inside, on the pretext of getting juice for one of the kids. I stand by the fridge and watch as she drags a kitchen chair to the side door and climbs onto it. Then, from deep within her T-shirt, she pulls out a string, on which a shiny key dangles. While the chair miraculously holds her weight, she stretches up on tippy toes to open a padlock that's hooked into a bracket. Then she climbs back down and pushes the door open with her hip. She has to open it quite wide to pass through, but she shuts it carefully behind her as soon as she's stepped inside. Ten minutes later she comes out and reverses the entire process.

"How many fish does your daddy have?" I ask Darren the next day.

"I dunno," he answers, shrugging. He jumps on his bike, pedals off, and shouts back, "Around two million."

I begin to position myself in the kitchen every morning at ten o'clock, to try to see inside the fish room, but no matter how hard I try, I never get more than a snippet. I try to have my eyes ready in different positions, but I just keep catching the same frame. I can see shelves and tanks, and sometimes water, but I never see any fish. Occasionally, something flickers, and I suppose it's a fish, but my glimpse is too short, and the lighting too dim, to tell.

I want to see more, but unless I can get hold of that key, I never will. The room is obviously top secret. I imagine Mr. Dwight towering over his wife, instructing her to keep the fish hidden, shaking his finger like a parent talking to a child. Maybe this is why he keeps her. She's his fish slave. There can't be any other reason, they're so mismatched.

～

ONE NIGHT, WHEN I'm in my room and my parents are sitting on the front balcony drinking their evening tea, I overhear them discuss me.

"I don't like her hanging out over there," my father says.

"Well, what do you want me to do? Run over there and pull her home? Cause a scene?" my mother replies.

"Can't you just tell her to stay home?"

"Oh, sure, you think it's that easy? You're not here, you don't know. She just goes while I'm busy with my clients. What can I do?" My mother's voice sounds helpless, as though my actions are propelled by forces way beyond her control, as unstoppable as gravity.

"Of course, I'm not here. I'm at work. What do you want me to do about that?"

My father fixes small appliances. I suspect that instead of fixing the toasters and coffee makers that cross his desk, he disassembles them and tinkers with their innards, trying to uncover the mystery of the universe among the wires. I've seen him do this at home, opening the iron or blender, tapping delicately with needle-nosed pliers, as though he's a heart surgeon. He'll ask me to pass him tools and explain things, as if I care.

Then my mother says, "I'm not happy, George."

"But you know I'm trying my best," my father replies. "We'll make one soon, you'll see." I can't imagine what they want to make. A machine that can make my mother happy? A supersonic vacuum cleaner, or robot duster?

"But soon I'll be too old," she says. "It's dangerous to give birth after forty."

My mother's words smack me. My parents are trying to make a baby. I can't believe it. Is it because they want a boy, someone my father can really turn into the next Einstein? Isn't his body too old? Don't the tubes and fluids for all those functions dry up? I know how babies are conceived, but to picture my parents trying to make one involves imagining my father taking off his gray suit and hanging it neatly on his special suit hanger. And then my mother, removing one of her neat blouses, and unhooking her stiff, wire-rimmed bra.

The rest is completely unthinkable, so I just tuck them both under the sheet, and force my thoughts to wander elsewhere.

I think about how my dad doesn't even seem to enjoy having me all that much. I'm like a puzzle he can't put together. I didn't come with an instruction manual, like some new appliance. A strong memory of my grade three Christmas concert comes to me. I was Rudolph and the rest of the class was singing my theme song as I pranced around, leading the team. I looked down at the front row, where my parents were sitting, and there was my father. I expected to see him cheering me on, but instead his mouth was wide open, and he looked completely baffled, like he had absolutely no idea what I was doing, like *Rudolph the Red-Nosed Reindeer* was the most complex story he'd ever had to follow.

I could operate my lightbulb nose by pressing a button hidden in my palm. The wire ran up my sleeve to a battery pack. I was supposed to give three quick flashes whenever the class sang the word *nose*. But when I saw my father, I stopped flashing. I was afraid my nose might be scaring him, that he might think I was about to be electrocuted.

The teacher was disappointed after the show. She didn't say it, but I knew I was the dullest Rudolph she'd ever put out on stage.

∾

THE NEXT DAY is Wednesday, my mother's varicose vein day. That morning, out of the blue, she asks me to go with her. She points to the back of her knees, to show me the progress of her treatments. The lines, which used to be bright green and purple, have faded now to light green beneath her white skin. She gets twenty needles in each leg. I imagine the magic liquid seeping in and spreading up the tiny streams of my mother's veins, cleansing them of whatever chemical stained them and made her look old.

"Sorry, Mom. I can't stand watching him give you those needles." I scrunch up my face to show her my disgust.

"But, Alberta, you don't have to watch. You can wait in the waiting room."

"Well, then, what's the point of coming?"

My mother's face falls. I feel a little twinge of guilt as she pulls on her straw sun hat with the yellow ribbon and picks up her matching yellow handbag.

She doesn't even turn to say goodbye at the door.

As soon as she's gone, I dress and run across the street to the Dwights'. Mrs. Dwight is already outside tanning.

"Good morning, dear," she says. "The twins are just

finishing their breakfast." She waves toward the door, like I won't know where to find them.

As always, when I enter the house, I fantasize that the fish room door will be wide open. Of course, this would spell disaster. The whole flat would be flooded in a minute. I can see the kids scooping up the fish in their fists, squeezing the life out of them, or biting off their heads.

I get the kids ready and put them outside, then I wash the dishes and clean the kitchen. The insides of the Dwights' cup-boards would give my mother connip-tions. They are coated in crumbs that stick to the residue of jam and syrup. As I work the hot soapy water, I imag-ine how thrilled Mr. Dwight will be to come home to a clean kitchen. I wonder whether the father of the family Camille is working for is anywhere near as gorgeous as Mr. Dwight. I hope he isn't. In my mind, I picture him grotesquely overweight and balding, and his breath reeks of garlic whenever he bends close to give Camille an order.

At ten o'clock, I wait for the heavy sound of Mrs. Dwight lumbering down the hall to the fish room. But she doesn't come. By ten-fifteen I think something must be wrong. Maybe Annie fell, and Mrs. Dwight is waiting for me to haul her up.

Suddenly, Darren gallops down the hallway. "Alby,

Alby, my mom, my mom!" he calls.

I drop the soapy rag and run after him. There on the balcony lies Mrs. Dwight, stuck between the chair and brick wall. She looks like one of those beached whales on a TV nature show, all flopped on her side and helpless.

I run up to her and fan her face with my hand. I can tell she's alive because her chest is rising and falling. I loosen the neck of her T-shirt, which seems to be choking her. It is then that I see the string. It will strangle her if it gets any tighter, so I tug on it lightly, not wanting to awaken her. When she doesn't seem to notice, I continue to pull until the key emerges from her cleavage. I lift the string gently over her face, loop it over the top of her head and let it slide against her damp hair until the silver key is nestling in my palm.

Then I run back inside and dial 9-1-1.

I don't know what else to do, so I sit on the ripped plastic chair and continue to fan her from time to time. Annie doesn't notice that her mother is gone. She continues her baby play, throwing around cheap plastic toys. Darren and the twins are standing at the bottom of the stairs, leaning on their bikes as though they can't decide what their next move should be.

When the ambulance finally arrives, two technicians begin to work on Mrs. Dwight. With impressive strength, they pick up her legs and arms and pull her out of the sun into the cool hall. Darren and the twins come up onto the balcony and huddle at the doorway, watching as their mother begins to revive. A technician helps her raise herself into a sitting position.

"Oh my," Mrs. Dwight says. "One minute I was watching the baby and the next thing I knew the lights went out."

The lights went out long before that, I think to myself. I want to expose her lie about watching Annie, but then she faints again. This time her head hits the hardwood floor with a great bang.

The three kids run to their mother, crying, "Mama, Mama."

"You'd better take these kids inside," one of the technicians says. "We'll need to take her in for a check-up. Could just be heat, but you never know."

I watch as they heave Mrs. Dwight's heavy body onto a stretcher, then load her into the ambulance. As he's closing the door, the other technician tells me to call her husband, and I nod to let him know that I will.

Then the ambulance drives off and I'm left alone, the entire Dwight clan, including Mr. Dwight, in my charge.

Just as the ambulance rounds the corner, my mother turns onto the street, returning from her varicose vein appointment. It seems so long ago that she asked me to go with her. She's walking slowly, the way she always does after her shots. I don't want her to know that I'm alone. I don't want her to think she has to help me. The thought of my mother in Mrs. Dwight's house gives me the shivers, so I settle onto Mrs. Dwight's plastic chair, and try my best to look casual. She looks over, just as I knew she would, when she's directly across from me. She waves slowly and I wave back, smiling as though everything is all right. Then she climbs the six stairs to our flat, holding the railing like a very old lady.

Alone, I corral the kids into the living room. They're a bit stunned by what just happened, even Annie. Darren switches on the TV, an old one that's thick as a car and sitting on a stand that has only three legs. The fourth leg has been replaced by old telephone books, the kind no one uses anymore, but it still isn't level and the picture of Big Bird dancing with Elmo is crooked. The three children pile onto the sofa and I squeeze Annie in between them.

"Watch her," I say, turning for the kitchen, my eyes on the lock to the secret room. My full view of Mr. Dwight's fish is just minutes away. But first, I have to call him. I take down the fridge magnet from his company and stare at the number for a few seconds, trying to decide what I'll say. I dial the number, hating the feel of my finger on the greasy buttons of the Dwights' telephone. A woman with a high-pitched voice answers, "Fortune Fences, bonjour, hello," and I quickly ask for Mr. Dwight.

"Who shall I say is calling?" the woman asks.

"It's Alberta. His wife's babysitter."

A few minutes later, Mr. Dwight comes on the line. His voice is deep and cheerful.

"Y'ello," he says.

"Mr. Dwight? This is Alberta. I'm over at your house, and, well, there's been an accident. Not an accident really, but Mrs. Dwight just went to the hospital in an ambulance. She kind of fainted on the balcony and they took her away. The kids are all here with me, but the ambulance guy said I should call you. I hope you don't mind." I blurt everything out quickly. Talking to him makes my knees shake.

"Oh, I see," he says, not sounding too surprised. "Well, I'll be there as soon as I can then. Thank you." He hangs up, leaving me standing with my heart thumping so loud I'm sure it can be heard all the way through the phone wires at Fortune Fences.

I know I have to work fast. Chaos is threatening to break loose down the hall. I can hear Annie whimpering, the twins fighting, and Darren trying his best to quiet them all by shouting, "Shut up!" every few seconds, which revs them up even more. Those kids aren't used to boundaries. When they play outside they're like tumbleweeds in the desert, rolling carelessly along, light and airy. Even on swings they keep wanting to go higher and higher, like they've never had anyone tell them it's dangerous.

Then I remember that I put some orange juice into popsicle trays in the freezer yesterday. I bring the treats down the hall and give one to each child. The popsicles fit into their mouths like plugs, quieting them. I tell them to be careful not to let the juice drip onto the sofa, even though it's already covered in grime.

I run to the back room, insert the key in the lock and turn it, taking a deep breath. As the lock slides out of the bracket, my heart races. Then I open the door and step inside. It takes a few seconds for my eyes to adjust to the dim. When they do, I discover that fish tanks are sitting on shelves that cover every wall. I open the blind a few inches to let in the sun, lighting up the room. All around me, fish are alive with motion, little bulbs of orange, pink, blue, silver, and yellow, some as small as my pinky, others big as my hand. Some are solid colors, others striped or speckled. They quiver constantly, their fins billowing and vibrating.

I walk around in a daze, staring into each tank. The fish's marble-eyes stare back from the sides of their faces, as if the fish know I'm intruding. They swim in and out of red-haired mermaids, gold treasure chests, sunken ships, and seaweed. In some tanks, tiny structures made of plastic-coated fencing are anchored in the pink and white pebbles. The fish swim elegantly in and out of the holes, as if they're weaving trails of invisible thread.

I recognize the wire — it's the same material that sits in bundles in the Dwights' backyard. Mr. Dwight must have sculpted these playgrounds for his pets. I can see him bent over the kitchen table, twisting bits of wire fencing into interesting shapes with his strong hands, working on each one as though it were a piece of art. He would have taken his time to think about each fish and what kind of playground it needed to make it happy. He must have done it when everyone else was asleep. That was the only time he'd have gotten any peace and quiet around here. I picture myself beside him, watching him work, passing him pliers or wire cutters. We'd work right through the night, getting so into it that time would actually slow down, until the sun came up. Then we'd laugh about how we'd never even noticed the time.

There is no way Mr. Dwight could share his feelings about these fish with his wife. Someone like her, with her stained clothes and bird's nest hair, couldn't appreciate anything this beautiful. The kids' room is still a mess of clothes and boxes. If not for me, they'd be eating on dirty plates with dirty cutlery. The other day I scrubbed the tiles in the shower with bleach, removing mold and uncovering their pattern of roses.

The longer I stare at the fish, the more alive I feel, as if they're charging me with electricity. They must have the same effect on Mr. Dwight. If they don't, he wouldn't take care of them the way he did, even building them playgrounds.

If only I could find a way to show him how much I like his fish. He'd be so happy to finally meet someone who appreciates them as much as he does. He'd put his arms around me and pull me close, surrounding me like a strong steel fence. I'd have no choice but to lean against him, feeling the beat of his heart. Then he'd bend down to kiss me.

I picture the kiss for a long time, so long that I start to get a warm feeling all over my body, like heat is travelling up my legs. When I imagine his hand brushing back the hair that falls on my face, my whole body shivers, like the fish.

The front door slams shut, startling me out of my daydream. It takes me a few seconds to move, then I run to the window and yank the blind back down. I leave the room and shut the lock, stowing Mrs. Dwight's key in my pocket. I wasn't expecting Mr. Dwight home so soon. I meant to clean the place up a bit, to show him what it could look like if someone just put in a little effort.

I can hear him with his children. They're talking over each other, trying to give him details of what happened. Thank god the living room is so far away down the dim hall. I'm sure he didn't see me. When I enter the room, all the talking stops. The kids and Mr. Dwight look up at me as though I'm an intruder.

"Oh, hello, Alberta," Mr. Dwight says. "Thanks a lot for looking after the kids. You can go now if you want to."

"Oh, that's okay. It's no trouble. I was just going to make some Kraft Dinner for lunch. I thought you'd want to go to the hospital."

"Oh, well, that would be great. Thanks. I'll call first, just to check."

I take all four children to the bathroom while Mr. Dwight phones the hospital to find out about Mrs. Dwight. I try to eavesdrop over the sound of running, splashing water and the kids fighting to be next to grab one of the many soap scraps that rim the sink. A sudden vision of my mother's own neat array of rose-shaped bathroom soap sitting in a cut-glass holder comes to mind. It wouldn't survive a minute with this crowd.

I don't know if I should ask about Mrs. Dwight. I

figure it would be best not to, if Mr. Dwight wants to tell me he can. Besides, I don't want to hear her name just now.

"Okay kids. The noodles are on," Mr. Dwight says, placing a pot of water on the stove. The kids all shout "hooray!" Mr. Dwight lifts the twins, one under each arm, and airplane-rides them into their chairs. Darren dive-bombs into his. I'm still holding Annie.

"Who wants milk, juice?" he asks. Hands shoot up. Mr. Dwight pours each child a drink.

"I can finish the macaroni and cheese," I say. I balance Annie on my hip, the way I've seen TV moms do, and pour the noodles into the boiling water.

Mr. Dwight gently nudges me aside, his hand on my shoulder. "I'll take over. Don't want Annie-Banany getting burned, do we?" The way he says "we" makes me want to burst.

I settle Annie into her high chair, then help Mr. Dwight at the stove. He scoops and I serve. Finally, we each take a bowl for ourselves.

"Well, bon appétit, everyone," Mr. Dwight says. The kids are already digging in, half-starved. They don't seem to find it strange that their father is the one feeding them, which makes me wonder if they're used to eating this way, with him in charge. For all I know, he does supper every night, while Mrs. Dwight vanishes to lie down somewhere. I wouldn't put it past her.

It's hard to eat in front of Mr. Dwight. My fork feels heavy, like it has to travel really far to reach my mouth. Between bites I look up at him. His blue eyes are so light, they remind me of the fish, with their slightly transparent bodies.

He doesn't look worried. I know what worry looks like from my parents. When they worry, the skin above their eyebrows creases. For all I know, Mr. Dwight is relieved that his wife isn't here. Maybe her insane laugh and dirty clothes get on his nerves too. In fact, this is probably the calmest meal he's ever eaten.

Whenever he catches my eyes, he smiles in a way that makes my stomach flip.

"Well, kids," he says at the end of the meal. "I don't want you to worry about your mama. She's fine. I called the hospital. She's just really tired. You know how that happens sometimes. She's having a good sleep, getting all rested up so she can come back and take care of you again. I'll go up and see her later, after she's had more rest. Okay?"

Darren and the twins nod their heads vigorously.

After lunch, we scoot the children back down the hall. Mr. Dwight tells them to watch TV. "You're not allowed out. Not without your mama to watch you," he says. I feel a jab when he says that, it's so ridiculous.

Annie is tired. I lay her down in her crib and she falls fast asleep.

"Let me help clean up, Alberta," Mr. Dwight says.

"Oh, you don't have to. I can do it."

"Oh, I'm sure you can, but I'd like to help."

Mr. Dwight scrapes the plates over the garbage while I fill the sink with soapy water. Every time he reaches over me to set a dish in the water, his arm brushes my shoulder. Then he picks up a dish towel and begins to dry. It all seems so normal, like this is our house and our family.

When he's dried the last dish, Mr. Dwight says, "Do you know if Angela fed my fish today? I know she usually sneaks down the hall to do it when the kids are outside."

"No, I don't think so."

Mr. Dwight pulls a key from his pocket and lets himself into the secret room, leaving the door wide open. I watch from the sink as he shakes food into the tanks, whistling. Fish rush up to the surface in a surge of color.

"Hey, Alberta! Do you want to come and see them?" he calls out.

Maybe this will be my chance to show him how much I like the fish. "Okay," I say, trying to sound casual.

Mr. Dwight pulls up the blind right to the top, fully illuminating the room. He points to the tanks and tells me their names. "We've got angelfish, butterfly fish, catfish, zebra fish, mollies, bumblebee fish, rubies, kissing fish, goldfish. You've got to be careful what kind you put together in the same tank. Mix the wrong ones and they just tear each other apart. Put the right ones together and beautiful things can happen."

Mr. Dwight looks at me and smiles. Our heads are so close, inches away from a tank that is lit by a blue bulb. It's like the glow puts us in another world.

Mr. Dwight takes my hand, very gently, and pulls me closer to the tank near the door. "Do you know what these are?" he asks. I shake my head, trying to calm my breathing. "These, Alberta, are gouramis. Those are kissing ones, with those huge puckered lips. They can grow up to a foot long, but not in this tank. I'll have to get a bigger one. These pearl gouramis look gentle, don't they?" He points to fish that are light orange, with pearly shapes and a horizontal black bar on their bodies. I nod.

"Don't be fooled. The males will tear each other to pieces, especially if there's a female in the tank." He stares at me hard, watching to see my reaction. When I don't say anything, he continues. "There's tetras in all these tanks. We've got glowlights, so called because of how they're so transparent." He points to fish that look plastic, except for bright orange and red stripes on their sides.

"And red-eyed tetras and silver dollars. Pretty things, but very shy. That's why I gave them so many hiding places." The tank he's looking at is loaded with rocks and driftwood. "I've seen them knock themselves out in a frenzy they scare so easily. That's also why their tank is high up, away from the kids' reach.

"Those orange and white ones there, shaped like discuses, are cichlids. They need very warm water or they die. Then the barbs here. Some of them are kind of vicious. You have to be careful what kind you mix. Like that tiger barb, or rainbow shark. Neither likes a communal tank. The loaches are a riot. The clown loach likes to lie on its side cause it's shy, but I think he's just giving a performance. You know? Playing hard to get."

Here, he lingers and stares at me again. I feel like he's waiting for my reaction, but I'm completely tongue-tied. All my intentions of telling him how much I love the fish are evaporating, or else they're stuck deep down inside me, hiding in a cave whose door is covered by a huge boulder.

"I've got some saltwater ones, but they're harder to do, so I'm starting off slow there. My favorite are these clownfish. They swim funny, more like a waddle." He points to a tank full of bright orange fish with white vertical stripes and mimics a waddle with his hands. The stripe around the fish's heads actually look like bandages, the kind you see wrapped around wounded soldiers.

"These tomato clownfish are really pretty, I think." He bends down and points at some fish that are bright red, with only one white stripe over their heads, like nurses' caps. A big shoe sits in their tank, with open holes where the laces would go. "Then I've got some rabbit fish too, but that's all the saltwater ones for now."

We wind our way right around the room, to the very last tank. The only fish Mr. Dwight hasn't introduced me to are little ones sitting in tanks high up on a wooden shelf, kind of out of sight. Maybe they're insignificant.

We just stand there quietly for a few minutes, watching the rabbitfish, which is kind of rectangular, mostly white but with yellow and black patches, swim in front of us. I can hear Mr. Dwight breathing beside me, expectant.

"Well, Alberta. What d'ya think?" he asks finally.

I think so many things I don't know how to express them all. I've never seen so much color and life in one place, all at the same time.

This is my moment. I have to show Mr. Dwight that I understand the fish and what they mean to him. I have to show him that they mean the same to me. I lean toward him, letting my shoulder touch his arm. Then I turn my face up to him.

"I think these fish are the most beautiful things

I've ever seen in my life," I say, my voice cracking.

"Do you? Well now, isn't that great. You know, not everyone feels that way about the fish."

"Yeah, I bet they don't," I say. He must be talking about Mrs. Dwight. I bet she barely glances at the fish when she feeds them.

I move closer, so close I'm almost leaning against him. My heart is racing. I imagine the blood in my arteries gurgling up from the deep like the bubbles coming up through the filter. Part of me knows it's wrong, but the way I feel about him is so strong, I can't stop myself. It's like there's some kind of cosmic force, stronger than gravity, pulling me toward him. And he must feel the same way. Why else would he want me here, with no one else around?

If Mr. Dwight kisses me, my whole life will change. The old me will be washed away, like yesterday's dirt. My life at home will change too because none of it will matter anymore — my parents can do what they want, they can have ten more children and their boring old lives won't affect me. I'll have this special thing with Mr. Dwight and they won't be able to stop me. Even Einstein knew that some forces, once set in motion, can't be stopped.

I lean closer, more heavily, against Mr. Dwight. I can feel each hair on his arm against my own. He shifts, as though to support my weight and help me settle in. But then, suddenly, he turns away and clears his throat, startling even the fish.

"Let me show you something really neat, Alberta, over here," he says. I follow him to a corner shelf holding a plain tank with nothing but a slab of rock in it.

"Know what this is?" Mr. Dwight asks. Two reddish-gold triangular fish are swimming inside, looking for something to do. Maybe Mrs. Dwight set this tank up and he wants to show me how pathetic it is.

"No."

"It's the breeding tank."

"The what?"

"Breeding tank. You know, where I put fish in to breed. These two are angelfish."

"I didn't know you needed a separate tank for … that."

"Oh yeah. It's really important. They need peace and quiet, away from all the other fish. They need to get to know each other."

"You mean, like a date?"

"Yeah, kind of," he chuckles. "See the way they follow each other around, like she's playing hard to get."

I nod, trying to stay cool, but blush anyway.

"Ah, you know something about that, I see." He stops talking and watches the fish for a while. "I've been using this same tank for years and it's never let me down.

Most of the fish in this room started off as fry in this breeding tank."

"Fry?"

"Yeah, baby fish. I guess you could say it's kind of like the honeymoon suite." Mr. Dwight laughs again.

Mr. Dwight and I are kind of in a separate tank right now, with the door closed, getting to know each other, just like the breeding fish. That dream kiss comes back to me, the one where Mr. Dwight puts his strong arms around me and pulls me close. It would be so easy to do. He's just inches away. And nobody would know. The kids are in the other room. Mrs. Dwight is miles away and my parents are across the street, probably fretting about me being here, but never imagining that I'm busy watching fish breed.

"Well now," Mr. Dwight says, clearing his throat. "Let me finish showing you how it works. You see that piece of slate in there?" he asks, pointing to the long, gray slab. "That's where the female will spray her eggs. She can lay as many as a thousand at one go. Then the male fish will follow behind and spray to fertilize them. It's a pretty easy system, don't you think?"

I can't believe Mr. Dwight and I are talking about ways to make babies, here in this magical room. My face must be scarlet, it's so incredibly hot in here. I don't want my father's voice in my head, but suddenly I can hear him talking about appliances. How the electricity charges them and turns them on. He says power creates more power, like a chain reaction. But it starts with one small move.

I reach out my hand and touch his, very lightly. It's like a spark igniting, my skin against his. He doesn't move away. He turns toward me. My lips are tingling, as though he's kissing me already. My heart is beating so loudly it's going to burst through my rib cage and smash the glass.

He opens his mouth and I brace myself, sucking in my breath. "Angela and I fell in love watching fish swim, at a pet store," he says.

I freeze.

"Now, we give each other fish for every occasion, birthdays, Christmas. The birth of our children. See those small tanks over there?" Mr. Dwight asks, pointing to the wooden shelf that he ignored earlier.

I can barely nod.

"Those are kissing fish. Angela's favorite. I get her a new tank every time she has a baby. I'll be getting her another one soon."

"You what?"

"I'll be getting her one soon. When she has the baby," he says.

"The baby?"

"Yeah, she's pregnant. Didn't you know? I thought she'd have told you by now. She always has a hard time being pregnant in the summer. She did this last time too, with Annie. Had to spend a few weeks in the hospital, out of the heat. I guess if we had air-conditioning, but we can't afford it. We put all our extra money into these fish."

Mrs. Dwight is pregnant. And Mr. Dwight sounds so happy. I thought he was going to tell me that she doesn't understand the fish. That she doesn't find them beautiful. That they don't strike her as graceful in the water.

I thought he was working up the nerve to move closer to me, to finally kiss me. But here he is, still going on and on about Mrs. Dwight, like I care.

"But Angela wouldn't want it any other way. We usually bring the kids in here at night, a sort of bedtime treat, you might say. Other kids might have video games or computers, but we want them to learn to love the fish as much as we do. You can't do that with those other things. They're just machines, not alive."

I see my father's dead machines, sitting on the shelves in his workroom. My dad spends all his time bringing them back to life, but I've never once been mesmerized by any of them.

"I get them all involved though, making our tank

decorations with scraps of fencing, plastic-coated, otherwise it's too corrosive. Certain metals can't take any bit of water. They rust up immediately, which, of course, would kill the fish. You've got to be really careful about ammonia poisoning too, the nitrogen and all that. They're finicky things, fish. Kind of like Angela herself. She needs all the right conditions when she's pregnant. The move was probably too much for her, all that packing and unpacking. We should've waited, but we needed more space and I thought it'd be better now than with a newborn. I blame myself, really."

As he's talking, I look around at the tanks and see the fence sculptures again. Except this time, they look stupid. They are nothing but scraps of lopsided metal, obviously put together by the Dwight kids.

"You've got to have the right filtration to remove the waste and you need to regulate the PH. The electrical hook-ups in this room alone are pretty phenomenal, but I keep all that hidden, behind the tanks. Cords for the lights and filters and ..."

Mr. Dwight goes on and on, sounding just like my father. I thought they were polar opposites, but now I'm not so sure. I didn't notice before, but the whole room is buzzing with the whir of electricity, like the room itself is plugged in.

It doesn't run on magic.

"Well, I guess I should go collect Angela now," Mr. Dwight says, finally coming to the end of his speech. In the dim light of the room I can still see his deep dimples.

But they mean nothing to me now.

༄

THAT NIGHT, WHILE my parents are outside drinking their evening tea, I sneak into their bedroom. It isn't a room I enter often. There has never been any frolicking together on the family bed, joking and laughing. There are no fascinating fish to marvel at. There's just the boring bedroom suite, with its matching night-tables and dressers, hers with mirror, his without. And in the corner, my father's suit stand, standing like another person, Einstein maybe in his early days at the Swiss patent office, tagging new inventions.

If a new invention is what my parents want, I'll help them get one. I still think their idea of having a baby is ridiculous, but I don't care. What does it matter that my father is old and my mother worries too much? If the Dwights can have another baby, why shouldn't my parents? The Dwights are just as annoying in their happiness as my parents are in their unhappiness. They're like mirror opposites, one on each side of the street.

I take out the key to the Dwights' secret room and slide it between my parents' mattress and box spring, on my mother's side. I push it in pretty far, so it won't fall out when she changes the sheets on Sunday. I hope it will work as some sort of fertility charm. There is magic in the fish room, just not the kind I hoped for. I can see the Dwight clan, cozy together in the secret room, admiring the beautiful fish. In the middle of them stands Mrs. Dwight, her belly rounded and protruding like a separate tank of its own, and inside it the little fry that Mr. Dwight gave her swimming about in its own fluid.

Back in my room, I pull my covers over my head and lie in the dark, listening to the sounds of my parents getting ready for bed. I think of Einstein's theory of relativity, or what I can understand of it, which isn't much. I see myself on that supersonic train zooming at the speed of light, taking me back to my childhood, back to when life seemed simpler. But that train will never exist. There is nowhere to go now but forward, into the rest of my teen years, and then eventually into adulthood.

There is no way to stop it.

Photography: Marilyn Gillespie

Lori Weber is the author of many books for young readers, including *Klepto, If You Live Like Me,* and *Tattoo Heaven.* Her acclaimed novel *Lightning Lou,* published by DCB, was shortlisted for the QWF Prize for Children's and Young Adult Literature. A native of Montreal, Weber lives in Pointe-Claire, Quebec and teaches English and Creative Writing at John Abbott College.

We acknowledge the sacred land on which Cormorant Books operates. It has been a site of human activity for 15,000 years. This land is the territory of the Huron-Wendat and Petun First Nations, the Seneca, and most recently, the Mississaugas of the Credit River. The territory was the subject of the Dish With One Spoon Wampum Belt Covenant, an agreement between the Iroquois Confederacy and Confederacy of the Ojibway and allied nations to peaceably share and steward the resources around the Great Lakes. Today, the meeting place of Toronto is still home to many Indigenous people from across Turtle Island. We are grateful to have the opportunity to work in the community, on this territory.

We are also mindful of broken covenants and the need to strive to make right with all our relations.